Louise Creighton

Life of Sir Walter Raleigh

Louise Creighton

Life of Sir Walter Raleigh

ISBN/EAN: 9783337333683

Printed in Europe, USA, Canada, Australia, Japan

Cover: Foto ©Raphael Reischuk / pixelio.de

More available books at **www.hansebooks.com**

LIFE

OF

Sir Walter Ralegh

BY

LOUISE CREIGHTON

WITH PORTRAIT AND MAPS

LONDON
LONGMANS, GREEN, AND CO.
AND NEW YORK: 15 EAST 16th STREET
1891

[*New Edition*]

" Hear him debate of commonwealth affairs,
  You would say it hath been all-in-all his study:
  List his discourse of war, and you shall hear
  A fearful battle render'd you in music.
  Turn him to any cause of policy,
  The Gordian knot of it he will unloose,
  Familiar as his garter; that, when he speaks,
  The air, a charter'd libertine, is still,
  And the mute wonder lurketh in men's ears,
  To steal his sweet and honey'd sentences."

SHAKSPERE, *Henry V.* Act i. Scene i.

PREFACE

MY object in this little book has been to gather round the person of Ralegh an account of the leading features of the age in which he lived, and by describing the events in which he took part, to show the work which Englishmen had to do in those days, and so briefly to tell the history of the time. I do not pretend to throw any new light upon any of the vexed problems connected with Ralegh's life. I have been much indebted to Mr. Edwardes's excellent collection of Ralegh's letters, and should like to refer anyone who wishes for further particulars about him to Mr. Edwardes's biography. For the general history I have followed mainly Ranke's *History of England*, Mr. S. R. Gardiner's *History of England, 1603 to 1616*, and his *Prince Charles and the Spanish Match*. Anyone anxious to know more of the history of James I. cannot do better than study Mr. Gardiner's excellent and most interesting books. Ralegh's own account of his voyages may be found in full either in the *Hakluyt Voyages* or in the Oxford edition of his works, where are also his political and other writings.

Schomburgh's edition of Ralegh's *Discovery of Guiana* gives the fullest and most accurate information, and to it I am indebted for my map of the Orinoco.

Mr. Spedding, in his *Life of Bacon*, vol. vi., treats at length of the circumstances which led to Ralegh's execution. The whole of the book is full of valuable information about the history of the time.

For the social history, Harrison's *Description of England*, at the beginning of Holinshed's *Chronicle*, and lately republished by the New Shakspeare Society, should be consulted. The *Sidney Papers*, and Sir Christopher Hatton's letters in Nicholas's *Life and Times of Sir C. Hatton*, give many amusing pieces of court gossip. A vivid picture of social life, and an interesting account of English literature under Elizabeth, will be found in Mr. J. R. Green's *History of the English People*.

CONTENTS

CONTENTS.

INTRODUCTION

IT is not always the men who have done most round whom the most interest gathers. There are some men whose individual character has had such force, that the impression which they produced on those amongst whom they lived has been handed down to the generations that have come after, and they have been remembered more for what they were than for what they did. The secret of the fame gained by such men lies in the fact that they have summed up in themselves some phase of human thought, or the tendencies of an age full of varied enterprise, or perchance have given the impulse which first directed human activity into a new channel. It is amongst such men that we must rank Sir Walter Ralegh. He is one of those who were great rather for what they were than for what they did. And this is not because he did nothing. On the contrary, he did so many things that we should find it hard to say in which part of his career he showed the greatest

B

eminence. But the interest attaching to him will always lie in this, that he exhibits the tendencies of a great age, of an age when men were stirred to new vigour by a sudden burst of intellectual life.

The men who gathered round Elizabeth were great in many ways, great as statesmen, soldiers, sailors, explorers, poets, and scholars. There was plenty of work for them all to do, and Elizabeth knew how to incite them to do it. She could put the right man in the right place, and make him do his best there. She made herself one with her people, and the secret of her strength lay in the fact that they felt she had made their interests hers. The people gathered round their Queen; and in the dangers which threatened Queen and people from without, they learnt a new sense of national unity. To study Ralegh's character is to study the tendencies of his age. There was no field of activity then open to men into which he did not enter; there was no work undertaken in which he did not share. In an age remarkable for its varied forms of intellectual vigour, he represents with wonderful many-sidedness the different interests which then absorbed men's minds. Moreover, whilst sharing so busily in the present, he looked on to the future, and discerned the way in which his country could grow in wealth and power beyond what any one at that time dreamed of as possible.

Ralegh's mind delighted in far-reaching schemes. Envious of the wealth gained by Spain from her colonies, he wished to see his own country benefited in the same way. He realized the advantages that England would gain by planting offshoots of her power in the new countries, with seemingly infinite resources, which were being opened up to commerce. He saw that the position of England and the character of her people eminently fitted her for the work of extending her power into distant lands. He never ceased to urge this upon his countrymen; he spent all his own possessions and his own health and strength in doing what he could to help the first beginnings of colonization. He gave the first impulse to the work which was afterwards carried out by others, and which has helped so much to make the England of to-day.

CHAPTER I.

Walter Ralegh's Youth.

WHILST Walter Ralegh was a boy, England was passing through years of great importance to her history. Even in his quiet Devonshire home there must have been much talk of what was going on in the outer world; of the Spanish marriage of Queen Mary, of the religious persecutions, of the new hope which filled men's minds at the accession of Elizabeth. Of these and such like things he must have heard his elders talk; but we know nothing of the immediate influences which affected his boyhood.

He was born at the manor-house of Hayes, near Budleigh, in the east of Devon, in the year 1552. Part of the house still stands, and is now used as a farmhouse; a picturesque old place, with three gables, heavily mullioned windows, and a thatched roof with deep eaves; surrounded by tall hedges and wooded hills. The Raleghs were a good old family, but neither very rich nor very powerful. Walter's father, also called Walter, had been thrice married. Walter was the second son

of the third wife, Katherine Champernowne. She
had been married before, and her sons, Humphry
and Adrian Gilbert, Walter Ralegh's half-brothers,
were in after years his associates in his schemes
of adventure and discovery. Their names are
remembered amongst the bravest of English seamen in the days of Elizabeth.

Devon produced most of the bold sailors of
those times, and its ports were filled with shipping,
and crowded with mariners returning from distant
voyages, ready to tell long tales of their wondrous
adventures. This cannot have been without influence upon the young Walter; for his home was
not far distant from the sea. We can picture him,
as a boy, watching with delight the busy stir of
the seaport towns, and listening with breathless
interest to the sailors' talk.

Some time in 1566, when he was fourteen
years old, Ralegh went to Oxford to study at
Oriel College. Under Henry VIII. much had been
done for the improvement of Oxford, and the
spirit of the new learning had given its studies
fresh life. Erasmus and Colet had introduced the
study of Greek, and Wolsey's magnificent foundation of the great college of Christchurch had given
a fresh encouragement to learning. Under Mary,
however, learning had again decayed, to be once
more revived in the burst of new life and energy
which greeted the accession of Elizabeth. Elizabeth herself was a good scholar, and watched
over the universities with fostering care. Just

before Ralegh went to Oriel, Elizabeth had visited
Oxford in state, and we are told that her visit
stirred up the scholars to follow their studies with
new zeal.   She was met outside the city gates by
the chancellor and doctors of the University, and
was greeted by a flood of speeches in Greek and
Latin.   To one of these, made in Greek, she
answered, after a show of bashfulness, in the same
tongue.   The next day was Sunday, and after
going to church in the afternoon, a Latin play
called "Marcus Geminus" was acted before her.
Puritan feeling was not yet strong enough to make
such an amusement appear a profanation of "the
Sabbath."   For four days the Queen stayed at
Oxford, and spent her time in visiting the colleges,
listening to speeches, talking kindly to the students, and advising them as to their work.   In the
evenings the scholars acted before her, and greatly
pleased the Queen and her courtiers.

Ralegh himself came to Oxford just too late to
see the Queen; but no doubt he found the students
still talking of her gracious behaviour, and of the
kind words with which she had bidden them
devote themselves to their studies.   He seems
to have distinguished himself by the eagerness
with which he studied, and the rapid progress he
made.

We know as few particulars of his college life
as we do of his early youth.   Lord Bacon tells us
one story about him.   He writes: "There was in
Oxford a cowardly fellow that was a very good

archer; he was grossly abused by another, and moaned himself to Sir Walter Ralegh, then a scholar, and asked his advice what he should do to repair the wrong that had been offered him. Ralegh answered, 'Why, challenge him to a match of shooting.'"

Ralegh left Oxford without taking a degree, and went in 1569 to France, that he might serve his apprenticeship in arms. By this time Protestantism had become a real power in Europe. The question which each nation had to decide in the midst of its internal struggles was which side it should take as a nation in the great conflict between Protestantism and Catholicism. In France the first struggle between the Huguenots, as the Protestants were there called, and the Catholics, had been brought to a close by the edict of Amboise (March 19th, 1563). But in 1567 the Huguenots rose again. They were alarmed by the successes which Alva, the general of Philip II., King of Spain, the most bigoted champion of Catholicism in Europe, had gained over their Protestant brethren in the Netherlands. Their first attempt was a failure, and for a time there was again peace. But in 1568 Alva offered to help the French King to put down the Huguenots, and war begun once more.

The Huguenots were aided in the struggle by the Protestants in the Netherlands and in Germany, and Queen Elizabeth sent them money. Elizabeth would not just then venture on open

war. Her own position was not strong enough
for that. In France and the Netherlands for the
time Catholicism was triumphant. At home,
Elizabeth was hampered by the presence of Mary
Queen of Scots, who had, in May, 1568, fled over
the border to seek safety in England from her own
subjects. Elizabeth stood alone as the champion
of Protestantism, and her first care necessarily
was not to endanger her own position. Still she
was willing to help the Protestants as far as she
could. She allowed her subjects on their own
responsibility to fit out ships to attack Philip II.
in his own waters, plunder his vessels and even
his colonies, and bring home from the Spanish
Main great store of booty. She did not interfere to
prevent bands of English volunteers joining the
Huguenot forces in France.

Ralegh went to France with one of these bands
of gentlemen volunteers. He was present at the
disastrous defeat of the Huguenots at Moncontour,
and must have seen much hard fighting, both then
and afterwards, when the Huguenots, in spite of
defeats, continued their stubborn resistance. They
gained no successes; but they showed that they
were too strong to be crushed, and got good terms
from the King, at the Peace of St. Germains
(1570). How Ralegh spent the next few years, we
do not know. He stayed in France amongst the
Huguenots till 1575 or 1576, sharing probably in
the desultory fighting that went on from time to
time. Peace between the Huguenots and Catholics

never lasted for long, and the terrible massacre of
the Huguenots on St. Bartholomew's Day (August
24th, 1572) made a lasting peace more impossible
than ever.

After he came back from France Ralegh lived
for a while in London. He made friends with
many of the gay noblemen who crowded to Elizabeth's Court; but he does not seem at this time to
have frequented the Court, or drawn upon himself
the notice of the Queen. He was much interested
in the schemes for colonization put forth by his
half-brother Humphry Gilbert. Humphry Gilbert
was one of the first to maintain that the love of
adventure which was leading so many Englishmen
to cross the Atlantic might be guided to some
better purpose than merely the annoyance of the
Spaniards and the acquisition of plunder. Gilbert
saw what England might gain by planting colonies
in some of those wondrously productive and fertile
lands which he had visited on the other side of
the Atlantic, and how new openings to peaceful
trade might in this way be found. Ralegh, who
was to do more than any other man of his time
to encourage colonization, from the first did all in
his power to aid his half-brother's plans.

In June, 1578, Queen Elizabeth granted Gilbert
a charter to discover and possess any distant lands
which did not as yet belong to any Christian ruler.
He was to plant a colony, which he was to hold
under the Queen of England. Many gentlemen,
and Ralegh amongst the number, joined Gilbert

in his enterprise; and he got together a fleet of eleven ships, which carried five hundred gentlemen and sailors. But from the very first the same causes of failure showed themselves that ruined so many kindred enterprises. There was no central authority strong enough to control the fleet. Each of the gentlemen who had joined it wished to have his own way. The sailors were for the most part criminals, who took to the sea to escape from justice—free-living adventurers, who only cared for piracy, and objected to all rule and order. With such materials it was hard to persevere through all the hardships and difficulties which must attend such an undertaking as Gilbert's. Some of the ships separated from the fleet immediately on leaving Plymouth. Then new disputes arose. Gilbert wanted to go at once to the North American coast to plant his colony; most of the others wished to begin by attacking and plundering the Spanish colonies. Gilbert was obliged to yield. On the way they met some Spanish ships. As always, a battle followed; for though Elizabeth and Philip II. might be nominally at peace, on the ocean at least there was ceaseless war between their subjects. In this struggle the English ships were worsted. The ships and the spirits of the men suffered so much by this discomfiture that at last Gilbert, to his bitter disappointment, was obliged to give up the whole undertaking, and return to England. He reached Plymouth in May, 1579, just eight months after he had left it, having spent all his money in this futile attempt.

How far the fleet actually got during these eight months, and what Ralegh saw on his first cruise, we have no means of knowing. For a time his mind was turned away from schemes of colonization to other interests. He was now twenty-seven years ·old, and had already seen much of life. His daring love of adventure had already shown itself, and that strong hatred of Spanish power and influence which inspired his whole life had taken deep root. After this we know more of the details of his life; for he began to draw men's attention upon him. Of these first twenty-seven years we know only the dim outlines. When he first comes clearly before us he comes as the fully-formed man, with strongly-marked characteristics and well-defined tastes and interests.

CHAPTER II.

Ralegh in Ireland.

RALEGH'S restless spirit did not allow him to remain long quiet after his return from Sir Humphry Gilbert's unfortunate expedition. In the beginning of 1580 we find him leading a company of a hundred men into Ireland to aid in the seemingly hopeless task of putting down the rebels.

Ireland was at that time in a most disturbed condition. Never since the country had been first conquered, in the days of Henry II., had order been made to prevail over the land. The efforts of the English rulers had soon been confined to the attempt to keep some order within the English Pale, as the district immediately round Dublin was called. Without the Pale the native chiefs, and the descendants of the Norman barons who had settled there when the island was first conquered, kept up a continual warfare for supremacy. The Norman families had adopted the manners and customs of the native Irish, and were as wild and uncivilized as they.

Henry VII. had tried to introduce some order; but he had hoped to persuade the most powerful of the native chiefs to own his authority by putting the government into their hands. The result naturally was that English influence grew weaker than ever. Henry VIII. could not rest content with such a state of things. He wished to make his power felt in the country by a firm and vigorous government, and at the same time to win over the turbulent chiefs, and make them adopt English civilization and order by seeing its advantages.

This policy might in the end have met with success. But one great cause of the continual disorders in Ireland has been, that no one policy has ever prevailed long enough to accomplish anything. The even advance of the firm though conciliatory policy of Henry VIII. was disturbed by the Reformation. As a matter of course, he introduced the same ecclesiastical changes into Ireland as he had introduced into England, re-garding both countries as politically one. No violent opposition was raised in Ireland either to the royal supremacy or to the dissolution of the monasteries; but when it came to changes in matters of doctrine, the case was different. The spirit of the Reformation had not influenced Ire-land at all. The people clung to the old faith, all the more vehemently because of the attempts made to force the new religion upon them. Catholicism was identified with patriotism, and

Protestantism and the English rule were regarded with equal hatred by the turbulent Irish chiefs.

In Mary's days, of course, the attempt to force Protestantism upon the Irish was laid aside; but it was taken up again under Elizabeth, and the religious question increased the difficulties of the Irish problem. There was no religious persecution; but it suited Philip II. and the Catholic party in Europe generally to suppose that there was, and so to use Ireland as ground from which Elizabeth's power might easily be attacked.

No means seemed more likely to bring order and civilization into Ireland than to encourage its colonization by English settlers. With this view confiscated estates in Ireland had been continually granted to Englishmen; but it was very difficult to get them to live on their estates, and it could hardly be expected that they would do so, unless some means existed to defend them from the turbulence of the native Irish. To maintain order in the country the presence of a large body of well-trained troops was necessary. This, of course, involved expense, and expense was the one thing which Elizabeth most dreaded. Economy was her passion; and though the result proved that her economy was most useful for the final good of England, yet at the time it often seemed to throw hindrances in the way of the wisest schemes of her servants. In Ireland especially, want of the necessary money prevented again and again the deputies from carrying out the

steps necessary to subdue the rebels and introduce order.

Of Elizabeth's deputies in Ireland none was so
successful as Sir Henry Sidney, the father of Sir
Philip Sidney. He took the office unwillingly;
and in his efforts to do his duty as deputy he met
with little encouragement from Elizabeth, who, on
the contrary, seemed always to throw hindrances
in his way.

He was at last successful in destroying the
power of Shane O'Neill, a great chieftain who had
done more than any other to endanger the English
rule in Ireland, and who had ruled as an independent prince in the north-western portion of the
island. Elizabeth had clung to the hope that he
might be won over to be a faithful subject, and
that she would be spared the expense necessary to
subdue him. At last she was persuaded to allow
vigorous measures to be adopted. O'Neill's entire
overthrow and subsequent death gave Ireland
some years of comparative peace; but soon new
causes of disturbance began to appear in the south,
in Munster, where a ceaseless feud raged between
the two powerful houses of Desmond and Ormond.

Elizabeth favoured the Earl of Ormond, because
he was a Protestant, and she hoped to find him a
useful servant in Ireland. The Earl of Desmond
had been dragged into a rebellion against the
English rule by the promise of aid from Philip
II. A force of about 700 Spanish and Italian
troops had landed at Smerwick, in Kerry, and

there on the shore built a fort, to which they gave the name Del Oro. Jesuits were busy stirring up the people to revolt, and the whole country was in a ferment.

This was the state of things which Ralegh found in 1580, when he landed at Cork with his force of a hundred men. He too had to suffer from Elizabeth's parsimony. We find him writing to the Lord Treasurer Burleigh, soon after his arrival, to complain that he had received no money to pay his troops, and had been obliged to pay them out of his own private means.

From the first Ralegh seems to have believed that nothing but the most vigorous measures, and the most ruthless severity to the rebels, would avail to bring order into Ireland. As it was, the Irish chieftains carried on a ceaseless war of pillage and spoliation against the English settlers. The English soldiers revenged their outrages whenever they could by worse crimes. There was no agriculture, no industry. All the resources of that fertile country were left undeveloped; and the English rule was once more seriously threatened by the great rebellion in the south, under Desmond.

Some months after his arrival in Ireland, we find Ralegh at Cork, acting as one of the commissioners who tried and condemned to execution as a traitor, James, brother of the Earl of Desmond, who had been captured in a chance skirmish. In August, 1580, a new deputy, Lord Grey de Wilton, arrived in Dublin. He was a stern and determined

C

man, and was by no means likely to shrink from severe measures. His first desire was to take the fort of Del Oro, where a new force of Spanish and Italian soldiers had just landed. Their commanders did all they could to stir up the Irish to make still more extensive plans of rebellion. The English were in continual fear of the arrival of a more formidable Spanish force, which they would be powerless to oppose on account of the small number of their own troops. To destroy the fort of Del Oro whilst it was still possible seemed the first thing needful.

Ralegh was one of the captains who accompanied Lord Grey on his march to Smerwick. It was a wild, stormy autumn; but the severe weather and the hardships of the march did not destroy the courage of the soldiers, nor the determination of their leaders. Whilst Grey attacked the fort from the land, Sir William Winter attacked it from the sea. The fort did not hold out for many days. Grey twice called upon the garrison to yield to mercy, but in vain. Ralegh was in the thick of the assault. On the three first days he led the attack, and also on the last day, when his troops managed to enter the castle and made a great slaughter. Then the garrison despaired, and hung out a white flag, crying "Misericordia!" "Misericordia!" But Grey would hear of no treaty, of no mercy, and the garrison were forced to make an absolute surrender. Grey's own words, in the despatch which he sent to the English Govern-

ment, best describe what followed. "I sent
straightway certain gentlemen," he writes, "to
see their weapons and armour laid down, and
to guard the munition and victuals that were
left, from spoil. Then put I in certain bands who
straightway fell to execution. There were six
hundred slain; munition and victual great store,
though much wasted through the disorder of
the soldiers, which in their fury could not be
helped." It seems that no lives were saved except
those of the officers of rank, who were distributed
amongst Grey's favourite officers, that they might
profit by their ransoms. The horrors of the
massacre are a clear sign of the bitter hatred
with which the English regarded the Spaniards
in those days. It may seem hardly possible to
find excuses for such cruelty. But we must remember how religious questions had irritated
men's minds; how Jesuits in disguise plotted and
schemed in England and Ireland, stirring up
men's minds to disobedience and revolt against
the government, even encouraging them to plot
the assassination of their Queen. In the excitement of their feelings, men believed the danger
from Spain to be greater than it really was; they
knew that the Spanish soldiers in Ireland and the
Irish rebels themselves shrank from no outrage,
however horrible, against the English; it was
hardly to be expected that they themselves would
treat the Spaniards leniently. It certainly seems
strange to see a man like Ralegh, afterwards the

refined courtier, the cultivated man of letters, engaged in such bloody work. It is only another
sign amongst many how he entered into the busy
life of those days in all its varied phases, and
gained experience of every kind.

The fall of Del Oro, and the massacre of its
garrison, was a death-blow to the hopes of the
Irish rebels. Desmond was pursued by the Earl
of Ormond, his hereditary foe and Elizabeth's
ally. His lands were wasted and pillaged, but he
himself escaped pursuit for three years, when at
last he was discovered hiding in a hovel, and was
murdered.

After his active service at the siege of the
Spanish fort, Ralegh was still employed in
Munster, where, in various skirmishes, he had
a good deal of severe fighting with the rebels.
Munster was in a state of hopeless disorder, and
Ralegh was disgusted with the inefficient means
taken to bring about a better state of things.
Active and clear-sighted, he was full of schemes
for the better government of the province; but
he and Lord Grey did not get on well together.
Grey seems to have been jealous of Ralegh's
abilities, and unwilling to listen to the advice
which Ralegh urged upon him, in the tone of an
equal rather than of an inferior.

In December, 1581, Ralegh was back again in
England. He was not silent either to the Queen
or to the Council about his views as to the state
of Ireland, and the inefficiency of the government

there. But the suppression of the rebellion had cost large sums of money. Elizabeth was fearful. of anything that might provoke another rebellion. Active resistance to the English rule was at an end for the time; but the condition of the country was no less miserable. Munster was utterly desolate. The corn had been burnt in the fields, the cattle had been slaughtered, the women and children burnt in their houses. Spenser thus describes the wretched condition of this part of the country: " Notwithstanding that the same was a most rich and plentifull country, full of corn and cattle, yet ere one year and a half they were brought to such wretchedness as that any stony heart would have rued the same. Out of every corner of the woods and glens they came creeping forth upon their hands, for their legs would not bear them. They looked like anatomies of death, they spake like ghosts crying out of their graves, they did eat the dead carions, happy where they could find them; yea, and one another soon after, insomuch as the very carcasses they spared not to scrape out of their graves; and if they found a plot of watercresses or shamrocks, there they flocked as to a feast for a time, yet not able long to continue there withall, that in short space there were none almost left, and a most populous and plentifull country suddenly left void of man and beast."

The power of the Desmonds was now at an end. Their lands, to the extent of half a million of acres, escheated to the Crown; and were granted out to Elizabeth's favourites as a reward for their services. If these lands had now been regularly colonized and cared for by resident owners, the benefit to Ireland would have been great. The lands were very fertile, and had great capabilities; but most of the owners were non-resident, and the colonization was irregular. Another golden opportunity for improving the state of Ireland was lost.

Twelve thousand acres of this land were granted to Ralegh. He clearly realized the good that might come to Ireland from colonization, and the profits his estates might yield if carefully managed. He took care to get industrious tenants, importing some from Devonshire and Somersetshire, and his lands were better cared for than most of those granted to Englishmen in Ireland. But Ralegh too was an absentee landlord. He paid occasional visits to his Irish estates; but as time went on his varied pursuits and interests hindered him from giving much attention to them. In 1602 he sold nearly all his lands in Ireland to Richard Boyle, afterwards Earl of Cork, in whose hands they became the most thriving estate in Ireland. It was on these lands that the first attempt at the cultivation of the potato was made. The colonists whom Ralegh sent to Virginia brought it back with them in 1596; and Ralegh, ever ready to profit by a new discovery, tried planting it first in Ireland, where it was to become such an important article of diet.

CHAPTER III.

Ralegh at Court.

BEFORE his return from Ireland, Ralegh does not seem in any special manner to have attracted Elizabeth's attention. We do not know how he first won her favour; but in those days it was not difficult for any young man to gain access to the court. Once there, a man's own wit and talents alone could gain him success. When Ralegh first appeared at court, Elizabeth was in her forty-eighth year; but she had not lost her love of admiration. She was still as much a coquette as she had ever been, and demanded as imperiously as any young beauty the entire devotion of her courtiers. There must have been much tinsel and unreality about court life when Raleigh first made acquaintance with it. The personal devotion which seemed natural enough when paid to a young queen of twenty-five, who was surrounded by difficulties and dangers, became absurd when directed to a woman of forty-eight. But exaggeration was the fashion, and no one could hope to get on at court who was not prepared to make-believe at least, by his words and actions, that Elizabeth occupied the first place in his heart. To the courtiers their behaviour to the Queen must have seemed a hollow mockery, a game which they were obliged to play, but which often became intolerably wearisome. We can well fancy how the gay young nobles who vied with one another in expressing their devotion and adoration to the Queen must, when the restraint of her presence was removed, have laughed together at the airs and graces of this faded beauty.

Ralegh began his court life under the powerful protection of Robert Dudley, Earl of Leicester. This man had long held the first place in Elizabeth's favour. He was said to have been born on the same day and at the same hour as the Queen. His appearance and manners were well fitted to charm her. She would have married him, had she dared to marry a subject, and probably no other man ever touched her heart as he did. She called him her "Sweet Robin," and allowed him much influence in her councils. She even forgave him what she regarded as an insult from any one of her courtiers, and what in him was doubly bitter, his marriage with another. Leicester had twice married; first Amy Robsart, whom he was suspected of having made away with, when he thought there was a chance of marriage with the Queen. When this proved hopeless, he married the Countess of Essex, in 1578.

The high position in which Leicester was placed necessarily made him unpopular, and his arrogance did not tend to diminish his unpopularity. He was intensely ambitious, and was willing to employ any means to gain his ends. It was said of him that he was prepared to poison or murder, in some secret manner, any man who stood in his way. Most likely he was suspected of more crimes than he actually committed; still it is true that at times people died most opportunely for his plans. He was supposed to have summoned a certain Doctor Julio from Italy to instruct him in the art of poisoning; and his victims appeared to die of natural diseases. Leicester's person was handsome and commanding, his manners were polished and affable; he was no ruffian, but possessed an absolute command of temper, and would have scorned to gain his ends by violence. His villany was not that of the rough Teuton, but of the astute and polished Italian.

Such was the man who, for some reason of his own, was now willing to further Ralegh's interests at court. In his position as favourite, Leicester seems to have feared no rival; but in council he was continually met by the stubborn opposition of Burleigh.

William Cecil, Lord Burleigh, was a man of a very different stamp to Leicester. He was now sixty-two years of age; and since Elizabeth's accession, first as Secretary, afterwards as Lord Treasurer, he had always been her chief adviser in State affairs. He was a prudent, cautious man, who had the interests of his country sincerely at heart. He served his mistress with a faithful devotion, which was never altered by the occasional harsh treatment which he met with at her hands. Elizabeth showed her wisdom very clearly in her choice of ministers, and she put great confidence in Burleigh. She respected his calm, deliberate wisdom. She knew that in the main she and her Secretary were of one mind in matters of politics, though her own caprice and temper often made her vent her wrath on him for the expression of views which her better judgment really approved. Burleigh himself had a high opinion of Elizabeth's capacities. He said of her that "there was never so wise a woman born. . . . For she spake and understood all languages, knew all estates and dispositions of all princes, and especially was so expert in the knowledge of her realm and estate as no counsellor she had could tell her what she knew not before. She had also so rare gifts as when her counsellors had said all they could say she would then frame out a wise council beyond theirs. . . . There was never any great consultation but she would be present herself, to her great profit and praise." To Burleigh it was intensely irritating to see how strong an influence might at times be exercised over the Queen's mind by any one of the crowd of favourites who hovered round her throne. Ralegh, introduced to the court by Leicester, must from the first have been an object of suspicion to the wise old minister.

But Ralegh's appearance at court excited still more bitter feelings in the mind of another man

who then occupied an important position about
Elizabeth. This was Sir Christopher Hatton, now
forty-two years of age, who had first of all attracted the Queen's attention by his beautiful
dancing at a masque in the Temple. He was the
one of all Elizabeth's favourites who seems to have
been most sincere in his love for her. Many of
his letters to her have come down to us. They
are the letters of an ardent and successful lover to
his mistress, rather than those of a subject to his
Queen ; and his love remained unchanged through
his life. Elizabeth herself was extremely fond of
him. Contrary to her custom with most of her
favourites, she rewarded his devotion with one of
the high offices of state, and appointed him Lord
Chancellor. He was a conscientious and prudent
man, and filled the office with credit. But no
reward could make up to him for the loss of his
mistress's love ; and he saw himself with despair
supplanted in her favour by Ralegh.

Ralegh's natural gifts, his courage and strength
of character, made him a formidable rival. Elizabeth was fully able to appreciate intellectual power;
and a man who possessed ability, as well as a fine
person, and an imperious manner which grew soft
and tender only to her, was sure to succeed with
her. How rapid was Ralegh's progress in her
favour may be judged by the fear and jealousy
which he excited in Sir Christopher Hatton as
early as October 25th, 1582, not a year after
Ralegh's return from Ireland. Hatton was then

away from Court; and he commissioned Sir Thomas Heneage to bear a letter from him to the Queen, and with the letter he sent three tokens. These were a little bucket, which signified Ralegh, whom the Queen seems to have nicknamed "Water," a bodkin, and a book. Heneage had some little difficulty in finding a moment when Ralegh was not by to give the Queen the letter and the tokens. He wrote to Hatton that she took them smiling, saying, "There never was such another." She tried to fix the bodkin in her hair, but it would not stay; and she gave it back to Heneage. After a while she read the letter, with blushing cheeks, and seemed to hesitate whether she should be angry or well-pleased. She ended by sending a long message to Hatton, veiled in the mysterious phraseology then fashionable. She said that if princes were like gods, they would suffer no element so to abound as to breed confusion; and that "pecora campi" (her nickname for Hatton) was so dear unto her that she had bounded her banks so sure as no water (Ralegh) nor floods should be able ever to overthrow them. As a token that he need fear no drowning, she sent him a bird, that brought the good tidings and the covenant that there should be no more destruction by water. But in spite of these and other reassuring messages, Heneage ends by saying, "that water hath been more welcome than were fit for so cold a season." All this seems absurd when we think that Hatton was a man of forty-two, and Elizabeth a woman of forty-eight; but his affection for her seems to have been sincere. Twice again, as his jealousy of Ralegh increased, did he send tokens and letters by Heneage to Elizabeth; and he is said to have died of grief for the loss of her love in 1591.

There were many other striking figures about the court when Ralegh first made his appearance there, and many must have looked upon the new favourite with disgust and envy; but most men were too full of other thoughts to be much occupied with him just then. It was in that year that the Duke of Anjou came to woo Queen Elizabeth, and all the world . was busy with the festivities which were got up in his honour.

This Duke of Anjou was son of Henry II. of France and Catharine dei Medici, and was brother of Henry III., who then reigned over France. For some time there had been talk of a marriage between him and Elizabeth. When he came to England the Netherlands had just elected him as their sovereign, hoping that by this means they would gain the help of the King of France in their struggle for independence and religious freedom against Philip II. of Spain. Once already, in 1579, the Duke of Anjou had paid a flying visit to Elizabeth. The marriage negotiations then seemed to advance favourably, and filled many of Elizabeth's courtiers and advisers with alarm. Amongst others she asked the advice of Sir Philip Sidney on the point. He was the son of Sir

Henry Sidney, who had shown such wisdom in the management of Irish affairs, and nephew of Leicester. He was the brightest ornament of the court : young, brave, and accomplished; a poet and a soldier; one of the first writers of pure and elegant English prose; and, what was rarest in those days, a noble and single-minded man, without selfish ambition or personal aims. He now dared to speak out his mind to the Queen on the subject of the French marriage. He wrote her a long letter, in which, in the most earnest and outspoken manner, he dissuaded her from a marriage with him whom he called "the son of a Jezebel of our age." Sidney's language was unmeasured, and fear of the wrath which it might provoke probably made him absent himself from court for a time. But he was there again on the occasion of Anjou's second visit, and took part in the jousts and tournaments which celebrated it.

Elizabeth really seems to have been very near marrying Anjou at one time; but though she professed to be very much in love with him, she can have been actuated only by motives of policy, by a hope that this marriage would strengthen her position against Spain. Anjou was twenty years younger than she. In person he was repulsive, of puny stature, with a face deeply marked by the small-pox, and a swollen and distorted nose. His character was thoroughly despicable. Though ambitious, he was mean and cowardly; though a bigot, he had no deep convictions; and he played an utterly ignoble part in history. Yet Elizabeth coquetted with him, and made love with him, as though he had really touched her heart. He was treated with every mark of honour and public respect. At one moment all seemed settled, and Elizabeth, in the presence of her court, after a great festival, drew a ring from her finger, and placed it on his. The opponents of the marriage were filled with alarm; but time passed on, and nothing more was done.

The Duke of Anjou spent three months in England in fruitless wooing, and then had to go back to the Netherlands. Elizabeth showed great grief at his departure, and herself went with him as far as Canterbury, where she parted from him with tears. She sent Leicester with a splendid following of nobles to accompany him to Antwerp. Sidney and Ralegh were both amongst the number; and fifteen vessels conveyed the Duke and his retinue to Flushing, where they were received by William the Silent, Prince of Orange, the great leader of the revolt of the Netherlands. On the 17th of February the Duke made his solemn entry into Antwerp. Splendid festivities followed, in the midst of which, no doubt, the English nobles found time to discuss deep and serious questions of politics with the great Netherlanders who were maintaining so noble a struggle for liberty. Ralegh stayed at Antwerp some time after his English companions had departed. He had a special mission from the Queen to the Prince of Orange, and the young man must have learnt much from his intercourse with this great statesman.

There was never again any prospect of Elizabeth's marriage with the Duke of Anjou. He behaved treacherously to ·the Netherlands by trying to set aside their liberties and make himself absolute ruler. He had to retire with ignominy, after the failure of a perfidious attempt to seize Antwerp, and died in Paris in 1584.

After his return from the Netherlands Ralegh continued to rise in Elizabeth's favour; but she did not give him what would most have pleased his ambitious and active mind—some office in the State, in which his restless energy might have found occupation. It was not Elizabeth's custom to reward her favourites with such offices. Probably her wise ministers, Burleigh and Walsingham, exerted their influence in preventing her from so doing. Besides, she seems always to have been guided by her own better judgment in the choice of her ministers, and to have allowed herself to be influenced only by the sense of their fitness for the post to which they were to be appointed. She rewarded her favourites in a manner more harmful to the country at large than to her own administration or to the royal treasury. Her habit was to grant them monopolies; that is, the exclusive right of buying and selling some particular article of trade.

She gave Ralegh licenses for the export of broadcloths in four several years; and in 1584 she granted him the " farm of wines ;" that is, the sole right of granting licenses for the sale of wines throughout the kingdom. In 1585 he was appointed to the important office of Warden of the Stannaries. The Stannaries were the tin mining districts of Cornwall and Devon. The miners possessed special privileges. There were Courts of the Stannaries, in which all their disputes were judged. The Warden had to watch over their interests, and sanction the regulations under which the mines were worked. Ralegh seems to have devoted much care to the duties of this office, which was by no means an easy one.

In 1587 Ralegh succeeded Hatton as Captain of the Queen's Guard. This gave him an important position about the court, and kept him constantly near the Queen's person. He received no pay but his uniform, the office being considered a sufficient reward in itself. The Guard was composed of men chosen for their good looks ; and the handsome uniforms in which they were dressed made them contribute greatly to the brilliancy of a court festival.

Gorgeous liveries were greatly in fashion in those days. Each nobleman was waited upon at court by a troop of serving-men in his own livery. The tilts and tournaments which were still the great amusement of the court gave the nobles plenty of opportunity for displaying their taste and fancy in dress. The courtiers rivalled one another, not only in feats of arms, but also in the

D

magnificence of the dresses in which they clothed their followers.

Shows and pageants of all kinds were in great favour. Queen Elizabeth was fond of making progresses through the country from the house of one noble to another, and each taxed his invention to discover some new way of amusing the Queen and her court. Elizabeth, though sparing in expenditure herself, liked her courtiers to be lavish in providing amusement for her. In 1583 she spent five days at Theobalds, Burleigh's country seat, when Ralegh accompanied her. She was so pleased with the entertainment she received that she told Burleigh "his head and his purse could do anything."

Her own love of magnificence showed itself very greatly in her dress. In 1600 her wardrobe consisted of 1075 dresses and mantles of different kinds, without counting her coronation and parliamentary robes. Most of her dresses were embroidered all over with different devices, covered with jewels, and adorned with lace of Venice, gold, and silver. She would appear first in a French dress, then in an Italian, changing the fashion of her dress every day.

It was customary that the courtiers should make the Queen presents every New Year. These, as a rule, consisted of articles for her personal adornment; either jewels or articles of dress. We find even the gentlemen giving her embroidered silk petticoats, and, still stranger, embroidere[1]

chemises of cambric.   Lawns and cambrics had
only been brought into England in this reign, and
became exceedingly fashionable for ruffs and cuffs.

These ruffs were one of the most monstrous
fashions of the time.   They were worn by men
and women alike, and were made of the finest
lawn or cambric.   They were at least a quarter of
a yard deep, and were made to stick out stiffly
round the neck, either by being starched or by
being supported with an elaborate arrangement
of wires.   Stowe, a historian who lived at that
time, says "that he was held to be the greatest
gallant or beau who had the deepest ruff and the
longest rapier."   At last Queen Elizabeth had "to
place grave selected citizens at every gate to cut
the ruffs and break the swords of all passengers,
if the former exceeded a yard wanting a nail in
depth, or the latter a full yard in length."

The women distinguished themselves by their
enormous farthingales, which were petticoats stuck
out straight from their waists, supported on struc-
tures of wicker.   To make the structure more firm,
they stuffed it with rags, tow, wool, and hair; and
the men stuffed out their breeches in the same
way.   The ladies covered their farthingales with
jewels and ornaments.   The ruffs also were orna-
mented with embroidery, and sometimes with
gold and silver lace.   Stubbs, a stern Puritan
moralist of those days, writes, "The women seem
to be the smallest part of themselves, not natural
women, but artificial women; not women of flesh

and blood, but rather mawmets (dolls) of rags and cloutes compact together." Both men and women painted their faces, and the beaux wore jewels in their ears. Perfumes were exceedingly fashionable, and perfumed gloves were introduced from abroad, and became a favourite article of luxury.

Ralegh, like the other courtiers, was fond of fine clothes, and liked to show off his handsome person to good advantage. He was tall, with a well-shaped but not too slender figure. He had a fine broad forehead, and thick dark hair; his complexion was clear and ruddy, but became bronzed in after years by his voyages and exposure to the sun and wind; he wore the pointed beard and moustache then fashionable. His eyebrows, which were much arched and very strongly marked, gave his face a slightly scornful expression, whilst his finely-cut mouth showed decision and firmness. Several portraits of him still remain, in each of which he appears clothed with great magnificence, and wearing many jewels, for which he had a great fancy. A contemporary writer says that Ralegh's shoes were so bedecked with jewels that they were computed to be "worth more than six thousand six hundred gold pieces." In one of his portraits he wears a suit of silver armour, and is richly adorned with diamonds, rubies, and pearls. Current gossip spoke much of his magnificence, and of his favour with the Queen; but his haughty manners and his success at court did not tend to make him generally beloved.

CHAPTER IV.

Ralegh's First Schemes of Colonization.

THE excitement of court life and his rapid rise in royal favour must have been very dazzling to a young man like Walter Ralegh. But the court did not absorb all his energies, and he continued to take part in Sir Humphry Gilbert's schemes of colonization, and to aid him as far as was possible.

For some time the energies of English explorers had been devoted to the discovery of a north-western passage to Cathay. About the wealth of this country of Cathay many wonderful stories had been told since the thirteenth century. It was a country to the north-east of China, inhabited by an active and enterprising people. Some travellers had found their way thither by land, and the wonderful stories they had told about the wealth which they had seen there had excited men's curiosity, and stimulated their avarice. At last, in the fifteenth century, encouraged by the discoveries of Columbus, men began to talk about the possibility of finding a north-western passage by sea to Cathay.

The first man who attempted this was Sebastian Cabot. He was the son of John Cabot, a Venetian, who came to Bristol as a merchant, and there, under the patronage of Henry VII., engaged in voyages of discovery in the Atlantic. Columbus was at about the same time exploring the West Indies. John Cabot directed his great voyage of discovery in 1497 more northwards than did Columbus, and saw the mainland of America a year before Columbus first sighted it. After his death, Sebastian Cabot, his youngest son, who had been born at Bristol, carried on his father's schemes of exploration. Still in spite of the courage and energy of the English explorers, they reaped no such rich fruits from their voyages to the coasts of Labrador and Newfoundland as did the Spaniards in more southern regions. But Cabot was convinced, as his father had been, that it would be possible to discover a new north-western passage to Cathay, and so open up a trade with that fabled land. His efforts to discover this passage failed, as those of so many others have done since. Still men were not discouraged, and others hoped for success where he had been unsuccessful.

An attempt was also made to find a north-eastern passage to Cathay. This led to the discovery, by Richard Chancelor, in 1553, of Archangel, the Russian port in the White Sea, and the opening up of the trade with Russia. A company, afterwards known as the Muscovy or Russia Company, was founded by a charter of Queen Mary in 1555 to prosecute this trade, and much interest in Russia and its inhabitants was excited. Still no one had reached Cathay. Belief in its fabulous riches had this good result, that it enticed men to endure endless hardships and perils in their pursuit, and led them to the discovery of new lands.

It was desire to find the north-west passage which made Humphry Gilbert first embark on his voyages. The scheme of finding out a passage to Cathay had been dropped for a time; but when he was only twenty-five years old, Gilbert began to do all he could to revive it. At first he met with little encouragement; but in 1576 he published a *Discourse to prove a Passage by the North-West to Cathay and the East Indies.* This writing helped to fire Martin Frobisher with ambition. He undertook in all three voyages with this object, and made many important discoveries in North America.

Though Humphry Gilbert had given the impulse to these voyages he took no active part in them, owing to disputes and jealousies amongst their organisers. His mind was, in consequence, directed to more useful schemes, to those plans of colonization which we have seen him trying to carry out in 1578, with the aid of Ralegh and others. Since then, the brilliant success of Drake's voyages had increased, if possible, the thirst for maritime adventure.

On the 26th September, 1580, Drake had sailed

into Plymouth harbour in the *Golden Hind*. He
had been away three years, and men had begun to
despair of his return. When he came back every
one was filled with excitement at the story of his
wondrous voyage; for he had sailed all round the
world, and returned laden with treasure which he
had won from Spanish ships in Spanish waters.
As England was then at peace with Spain, these
doings were no better than piracy. But in spite
of the complaints of the Spanish Ambassador,
Elizabeth took no steps to punish Drake. On
the contrary, when he brought the *Golden Hind* to
Deptford, she allowed him to entertain her on
board at a splendid banquet, and on that occasion
knighted him for his great prowess. It is said,
that of the treasure brought home by Drake, he
was allowed to keep £10,000 for himself, whilst
£60,000 in jewels and money was safely lodged
in the Tower. It is not strange that the wrath of
the Spanish king, Philip II., was great at the loss
of this treasure, and at the insult offered to his
power. Elizabeth affected to restrain, but in truth
connived at, the piratical expeditions of her subjects in the Spanish seas. English vessels sailed
into Spanish ports in South America, plundered
and burnt the ships lying in the harbours, and in-
tercepted Spanish vessels bringing home treasure
from the colonies. In all this the English ran
terrible risks. If they failed, they were treated
as pirates, for their Queen was at peace with the
Spanish king. They were killed without mercy,

or subjected to lingering tortures by the Spanish Inquisition. Still the gain was great enough to make men willing to face the risk; and hatred to Spain was increased by the tales of the horrible sufferings inflicted upon English seamen by the Spaniards. Elizabeth had difficulty in keeping the animosity of her subjects within bounds. She always hoped to prevent an open rupture with Spain, or at least to put it off as long as possible, that in the meanwhile she might gain strength and increase her resources. Her policy was to play off France against Spain, and to give enough help to the revolted Netherlanders to enable them to go on with their struggle, so that Spain might be kept busy by them. In the meanwhile she allowed her subjects to help to fill her treasuries with Spanish gold, so that she might have the means to prepare for the struggle if it should come.

We have seen how some of the English seamen were animated by a desire to discover a north-western passage to Cathay, others by hatred of the Spaniards and love of Spanish treasure; others again, though as yet only a small body, by a desire to found English colonies in America, and so to open up a new trade which might be as profitable to England as the trade with New Spain was to the Spaniards. In 1583, Sir Humphry Gilbert made a second attempt to plant a colony in Newfoundland. He was not rich enough to undertake the expedition solely at his own expense, and so got others to share with him the risks and possible

profits of the expedition. Ralegh contributed a
vessel, the barque *Ralegh*, and Gilbert sailed from
Plymouth harbour on the 11th June, 1583, with a
little fleet of five vessels.   Before leaving, Gilbert
received a letter from Ralegh, who sent him a
token from the Queen, an anchor, guided by a
lady, and conveyed to him her wishes for his
welfare, adding that she desired him to leave his
portrait for her.

Gilbert had hardly left Plymouth when he was
deserted by the barque *Ralegh*, on the plea of ill-
health amongst the crew, which seems to have
been only an excuse.   The rest of the little fleet
proceeded on their way.   At first Gilbert seemed
to meet with success, but his colony failed for
the same reasons that so many other schemes of
colonization failed in those days.   The men were
for the most part lawless adventurers, some of
them pirates and robbers.   They wanted to make
their fortunes at once.   They lacked the perse-
verance, the industry, the patient endurance of
hardships, which alone can surmount the difficulties which beset the first planting of a colony.
Everything went wrong, and at last the men
clamoured to be taken home.   Gilbert was forced
to consent, and to abandon, at least for a time, his
cherished scheme.   He hoped to do a little in the
way of exploring the coast on his way home, and
left one ship to carry the sick direct to England.
Another of the ships struck on a rock, and was
lost with more than a hundred men.   Then the

rest of the men grew still more discontented, and insisted on being taken home at once. Gilbert was in the smaller of the two ships left, a little. vessel called the *Squirrel*, of only ten tons burden. It was not thought to be seaworthy; still he would not listen to any persuasions to leave it, but answered, "I will not forsake my little company going homeward, with whom I have passed so many storms and perils." They met with very foul weather, but Gilbert kept up his spirits; and when the other vessel, the *Golden Hind*, drew near the *Squirrel*, he cried out to its crew, "We are as near to heaven by sea as by land." That night the *Squirrel* was on ahead, when suddenly the crew of the *Golden Hind* saw her lights disappear, and nothing more was ever seen or heard of Sir Humphry Gilbert. The *Golden Hind* reached Falmouth on the 22nd September, some three months after the starting of the expedition.

It was left to Sir Walter Ralegh to pursue his schemes of colonization alone. In March, 1584, Elizabeth gave him a charter, authorizing him and his heirs to discover and take possession of any lands not actually possessed of any Christian prince. He and his heirs were to have the right of governing in perpetuity any colony founded within the next six years. Ralegh did not turn his attention to the cold districts where Gilbert had tried to found his colony; he wished to explore more southern regions. He fitted out and despatched two barks, under Captains Philip Ama-

das and Arthur Barlowe, with orders to explore
the coast north of Florida. The fertility of this
district had been discovered some time before by
the French. They had called it Carolina in honour
of Charles IX.; and some French Huguenots had
tried to plant a colony there, which had been
destroyed by the Spaniards, who massacred 200
men, women, and children.

It was probably when engaged in the civil wars
in France that Ralegh heard tell of the wondrous
fertility of these lands; and when he matured his
schemes of founding a colony, it was to this coast
that he turned his attention. Amadas and Barlowe
had a very successful voyage, of which they have
left a narrative. As they drew near the coast they
smelt "so sweet and so strong a smell as if they
had been in the midst of some delicate garden."
For 130 miles they sailed along the coast before
they found an entrance; then they landed on the
Island of Wocoken, the southernmost of a group
of islands in Pamlico Sound, and took possession
of it in Queen Elizabeth's name. This island was
so full of grapes "that the very beating and surge
of the sea overflowed them." The vines covered
the ground everywhere, and climbed towards the
tops of high cedars. The island had also "many
goodly woodes, full of deer and hares; the trees
were chiefly cedars, and all manner of spice-bearing
trees." After three days some of the natives appeared, and one came on board the ship willingly
and without any fear. The next day many more

came; "very handsome and goodly people, and in their bearing as mannerly and civil as any of Europe." They had friendly intercourse with the natives, and trafficked with them, exchanging tin and copper dishes for skins and dyes. After some days a few of the English ventured further up the creek, and found an island, Roanoake by name, where was a small native village. Here they were received most hospitably. The women washed their clothes, and prepared a solemn banquet for them. Roanoake was sixteen miles long, and there were many other islands in the group, all fertile and covered with goodly trees; "the soile the most plentiful, sweete, fruitfull, and wholesome of all the world." Amadas and Barlowe explored no further, but returned to England about the middle of September; and Ralegh was well satisfied with the report they brought him. Queen Elizabeth christened the new district Virginia, that it might always bring back to men the memory of their virgin Queen; and Ralegh set about at once to plan a larger expedition, which was to plant a colony in his new possessions.

Ralegh did not venture to lead this expedition himself. He was afraid to leave Court lest he should give his enemies opportunities to conspire against him. Leicester, his former patron, had grown bitterly jealous of his favour with the Queen. The expedition was therefore entrusted to Ralph Lane and Sir Richard Grenville, both men who had led stirring lives, and taken part in

Irish and Continental wars. They left Plymouth on the 9th April, 1585, taking with them Barlowe and Amadas as pilots. Neither Grenville nor Lane were fitted for the arduous task before them. Grenville was bold and impetuous, and had learnt from the Spaniards to treat the natives with cruelty, regarding them only as people to be robbed. He wanted to grow rich, either by gaining booty from the Spaniards or by robbing the natives. On the way he loitered about the seas, hoping to fall in with Spanish vessels, and when he reached Virginia, on the 26th June, he did nothing to help the colonists. His treatment of the natives may be judged by the account left of this voyage, in which, after stating that they were well entertained by the natives, the writer goes on to add: "One of our boats with the Admiral was sent to demand a silver cup which one of the savages had stolen from us, and not receiving it according to his promise, we burnt and spoiled their corn and town, all the people being fled."

Grenville also managed to quarrel with Lane, and after spending seven weeks in exploring the coast, returned to England.· On the way back he captured a Spanish vessel of 300 tons, richly laden, and reached Falmouth on the 6th October.

Lane was left alone in Virginia with a hundred men. Grenville promised to return to them early in the next spring with new colonists and stores of provisions.

Ralph Lane was no better fitted than Grenville

to found a colony. He determined to establish himself on the Island of Roanoake, and built a fort which he called Port Ferdinando; but he built no dwelling-houses, he sowed no corn, and made no arrangements for supplying his colonists with provisions, but trusted to the Indians to do everything for them. He writes in enthusiastic terms of the island, calling it "the goodliest isle under the cope of heaven, so abounding with sweete trees that bring such sundry rich and pleasant gums, grapes of such greatness, yet wilde, as France, Spain, nor Italy have no greater. . . . The climate so wholesome that we had not one sick since we touched the land here. . . . The people naturally are most courteous." Yet he made no attempt to profit by this extraordinary fertility. His one idea seems to have been to explore the country with a view of finding mines. He was led on by a tale told him by the natives of a country where a soft pale metal, either copper or gold, was to be found in such quantities that the people beautified their houses with great plates of it. But he was obliged to return before he reached this land of promise, on account of the failure of his provisions. He looked upon this as the most important part of his proceedings; for he said, "The discovery of a good mine, by the goodness of God, or a passage to the South Sea, or some way to it, and nothing else, can bring this country in request to be inhabited by our nation." This remark shows how unfit the adventurers were to found a colony by patient labour, even in a land where nature was most bountiful.

Meanwhile the colonists, who stayed at the Fort whilst Lane explored, had been ill-treating the friendly natives. They behaved to them as though they were their slaves, and soon aroused their resentment. The natives too began to be less afraid of the white men, since they saw that "their Lord God suffered them to sustaine hunger." The chief friend of the colonists amongst the natives died; and the natives, wearied of the hard usage they received, plotted to destroy their taskmasters. Their plan was to refuse, first of all, to supply them with provisions. They foresaw that want would disperse the white men in search of food, when they would be more easily able to kill them. In truth, when the native supplies were withdrawn, the colonists were so hard pressed for food that Lane had to disband his company into sundry places to live upon shell-fish. Lane's vigilance, however, prevented the plots of the natives from being successful. When it came to a trial of strength, their superior arms gave victory to the white men, and the natives fled, whilst their king was left amongst the slain.

This happened on the 1st of June, 1586; but as Grenville had never returned with his promised stores, it would have gone hard with the colonists had not chance brought them a welcome friend.

On the 8th of June, Lane was told that a fleet

of twenty-three sail had been sighted; but whether friend or foe, was not known. The next day it was discovered that Drake himself was the leader of this fleet. He was returning laden with booty from a piratical expedition to the Southern Seas, and touched at Roanoake to visit the English colony there. He was most friendly to his countrymen in their distress. At first Lane asked him to carry the weak men among the colonists to England, and leave him some new hands, with provisions and shipping to carry them to England in August, by which time he hoped to have finished his exploration of the country. But a terrible storm seems to have frightened the colonists, and with one voice they asked Lane to beg Drake to take them all back to England with him. To this request Drake readily assented; and on the 19th of June they set sail, and the colony was deserted.

Very soon after their departure, a ship which Ralegh had sent off, laden with provisions and stores for their relief, arrived at Virginia. Not finding the colonists, it returned at once to England. A fortnight after it had left, Sir Richard Grenville arrived with three ships, fitted out also for the relief of the colonists. He travelled into divers parts of the country to see if he could hear any news of their colony; but he found " the places which they had inhabited desolate." They had "left all things confusedly, as if they had been chased from thence by a mighty army." "And no doubt so they were," adds the chronicler

E

of the voyage; "for the hand of God came upon them for the cruelty and outrages committed by some of them against the native inhabitants of that country."

Grenville was unwilling "to lose the possession of that country which Englishmen had so long held;" so he left fifteen men at Roanoake, furnished well with provisions, and set sail for England again.

Sir Walter Ralegh's first attempt at a colony had failed; but he did not on that account give up his plans. Some among the men who had shared in the expedition were fully convinced of the advantages which might be reaped from colonizing Virginia. One of these, Thomas Hariot, wrote a long letter to tell men the truth about this enterprise, seeing that it had been very "injuriously slandered." He sums up the causes of the failure of the expedition, and makes them consist in the characters of the men who had undertaken it. Some, he says, "after gold and silver was not so soon found as was by them looked for, had little or no care of anything else but to pamper their bellies." Some had "little understanding, less discretion, and more tongue than was needfull or requisite." Others again, "because there were not to be found any English cities, nor such fair houses, nor at their own wish any of their old-accustomed dainty food, nor any soft beds of down or feathers, the country was to them miserable, and their reports thereof accordingly." Hariot goes on to enumerate all the varied and rich products of Virginia. Amongst these products was one which, once brought to England, rapidly gained favour. "There is an herbe which is sowed apart by itself, and is called by the inhabitants Yppowoc. . . . The Spaniards generally call it tobacco. The leaves thereof being dried and brought into powder, they used to take the fume or smoke thereof by sucking it through pipes made of clay into their stomach and head. . . . We ourselves, during the time we were there, used to suck it after their manner, as also since our returne, and have found many rare and wonderful experiments of the vertues thereof, of which the relation would require a volume by itselfe. The use of it by so many of late, men and women of great calling, as else, and some learned physicians also, is sufficient witness."

Ralegh himself seems soon to have become fond of this new luxury. He used pipes of silver instead of pipes of clay. On one occasion it is said that a servant, who was bringing him some ale, was so terrified at seeing him smoking that he threw the ale over him, and ran down stairs, shouting that his master was on fire. We do not know whether Elizabeth ever tried the effects of tobacco herself, but she would sit by Ralegh whilst he smoked. One day she said to him, that however clever he might be, he could not tell the weight of the smoke from his pipe. When Ralegh affirmed that he could do so, the Queen remained

incredulous, and made a bet against him.   Ralegh
showed his ingenuity by weighing first a pipeful
of tobacco; then, when he had smoked the pipe,
he weighed the ashes that remained, and demonstrated to Elizabeth that the difference between
the two weights was the weight of the smoke.
Elizabeth was convinced, and paid the bet.

But Ralegh believed that he could get more
from Virginia than a new luxury.   He had spent
a great deal of money in these unsuccessful attempts; but the Spanish prizes brought home by
Grenville more than compensated for the outlay.
In 1587 he was ready to fit out a new expedition.
He placed a certain Captain Charles White at the
head of it, and sent three ships, with a hundred
and fifty colonists on board, among whom were
seventeen women and nine children.   The presence of the women gave reason to hope that the
colony might be more successful this time; for
men who had their wives and children with them,
would be impressed with the need of settling down
and making homes for themselves, before they
hunted for treasure.

The expedition left Plymouth on the 8th May,
1587.   From the first White seems to have been
thoroughly in earnest about his task; but the
men with whom he had to work were not always
willing to obey and listen to him.   His first object
on reaching Virginia was to look for the fifteen
colonists left there by Grenville on the Island of
Roanoake; but he found "none of them, nor any

sign that they had been there, saving only they found the bones of one of those fifteen." When they reached the spot where Lane had built his fort, they found the fort razed down, but all the houses standing unhurt, "saving that they were overgrown with melons of divers sorts, and deer within them feeding on these melons." Then they gave up hope of ever seeing any of these fifteen men alive.

White's intention had been to advance, according to instructions given by Ralegh, as far as Chesapeake Bay, rather further north, and settle down there; but a man named Ferdinando, who seems to have opposed White as much as possible in everything, and who had chief command of the vessels, refused to go on any further with the colonists, and landed them all at Roanoake. So White gave orders that they should repair the houses already standing there, and build some others. White was anxious to renew friendly relations with the natives; but they had been made suspicious by the behaviour of the former colonists. At last, however, he succeeded in having a conference with some of them, who told him how the fifteen colonists left by Grenville had been surprised and killed. White thought it right to revenge the death of his fellow-countrymen, and attacked and killed some of the natives, which did not tend to increase their friendly feeling to the white men.

On the 18th of August Elinor Dare, White's

daughter, and wife of one of the colonists, gave birth to a daughter, who, as she was the first Christian child born in the colony, was named Virginia. The ships which had brought the colonists over now began to make ready to return to England. White wished to stay behind; but the colonists earnestly besought him to return to England, that he might obtain supplies for them. He at last yielded to their entreaties and set sail for England, which he reached on the 5th November.

About this time Ralegh's interest in his Virginian colony seems to have flagged a little. Possibly he had more important things to think about. His influence at Court had increased, and he must have found Court intrigues very engrossing. Besides, all England was then in expectation of a Spanish invasion, and men were busy with preparations to meet it. But White had the interest of the colony, where he had left his daughter, sincerely at heart. He was, as he says himself, "sundry times chargeable and troublesome unto Ralegh for the supplies and reliefes of the planters in Virginia."

All that White could at last obtain was, that three vessels, going out to gain wealth by piracy in the West Indies, should take him with them to Virginia. But the ships refused to carry any supplies for the colonists, and took only White himself and his chest. He sailed from Plymouth on the 20th March, 1590, and did not reach Virginia till 17th August. Seeing a great fire near

the shore, White writes, "we sounded with a trum-
pet a call, and afterwardes many familiar English
tunes of songs." But there were no Englishmen
there to be gladdened by the welcome sound ; only
savages, who fled at their approach. When White
reached the group of houses where he had left the
colonists, he found everything in a state of desola-
tion; but he found no sign of distress, such as they
had promised to leave, should they be driven to
extremities. At last he found carved on a tree,
from which the bark had been partially removed,
the word Croaton, in fair capital letters. This he
took to mean that the planters had departed to
Croaton. He found five chests, which had been
carefully hidden, but had been discovered and
plundered by the savages, who had found the con-
tents for the most part of little good to them.
They had consequently left them—books, maps,
and pictures—lying about, torn and rotted with the
rain. White would gladly have gone on to Croaton
to search for the colonists, but he could not persuade the captains of the ships who had brought
him to Virginia to do so, and so had to return to
England with them.

Ralegh fitted out no more expeditions to Virginia. It is indeed wonderful that, with only the
means of a private gentleman, he should have per-
severed so long in so formidable a task. Already,
in 1589, he had transferred the patent given him
by the Queen to a company of merchants. They
made no use of it; but in 1602 it passed to a more

energetic company, who at last, in 1606, began the real colonization of Virginia, for which Ralegh had paved the way. The new colonists heard that the people left by White had been miserably slaughtered; some however had escaped and gone far inland, where they lived peaceably with the natives. It was reported that there were still seven English alive, four men, two boys, and one maid; but the new settlers never found them.

CHAPTER V

The Spanish Armada.

THE time had now come when Philip II. determined to make an open attack upon England. In 1587, Elizabeth had at last been persuaded to consent to the execution of Mary Queen of Scots. Since her flight from Scotland in 1568, Mary had been kept in prison in England for nineteen years altogether; and she had been a centre round which discontent could always gather. Plots had been formed with the object of restoring her to liberty, making her Queen of England, and bringing back the Catholic religion. Philip II. had often threatened to interfere on her behalf.

By the execution of Mary, Elizabeth removed the object of endless intrigues at home and abroad. Henceforth the real question of the day was clearly set before the minds of all Englishmen. But Mary's execution hurried on the plans of Philip II. So long as Mary lived, Philip could only interfere in Mary's behalf. Now that she

was dead, he could go forth to conquer England
in his own name.   Hitherto he had hoped to re-
duce the Netherlands first, and thence proceed to
re-establish Catholicism in England.   But he found
England in the way of his plans.   English help
had encouraged the Huguenots to carry on their
resistance in France; English gold had helped
Philip's revolted subjects in the Netherlands;
English seamen had again and again robbed him
of his treasure.   Philip determined to alter his
plans.   England was the key to the Protestant
resistance in Europe.   England must be entirely
crushed before he could succeed in striking a
death-blow to Protestantism.   To Englishmen the
problem was made simple by the attitude of
Philip.   English Catholics, or other malcontents,
were willing enough to fight for Mary Queen of
Scots; but they would fight for Elizabeth rather
than see their country crushed by Philip.

Philip's preparations were delayed by the reckless daring of Drake, who, in 1587, led a fleet of
twenty-five sail into the harbour of Cadiz, with
the view of "singeing King Philip's beard," as he
said.   There he found sundry great ships laden
with provisions for the projected invasion of England.   He sank some thirty-four ships, and carried
away four more with him, and did other damage
on the coasts of Spain and Portugal.   So Philip's
preparations were delayed; and though he set
to work with new vigour to fit out a mighty
fleet, which should once for all crush these im-

pudent islanders, it could not be got ready before June, 1588.

This fleet, "the most fortunate and invincible Armada," consisted of 132 ships, manned by 8,766 sailors and 2,088 galley slaves, and carrying 21,855 soldiers. Alexander, Prince of Parma, who was now Spanish Commander in the Netherlands, and the greatest general of the age, was to join the fleet in the Channel with 17,000 Spanish troops from the Netherlands, so that there might be an army of 50,000 men for the invasion of England.

Meanwhile Elizabeth could not believe in the danger which was threatening her. It seems as if both she and Burleigh had hoped, up to the last moment, that they would be able to avert it by negotiations. Both the army and the navy were in a thoroughly unfit state to meet the invaders. The Lord High Admiral, Lord Howard of Effingham, was in despair, and wrote to Walsingham and Burleigh begging for reinforcements, and complaining bitterly of the condition of the navy.

In one thing the English people were strong, and that was in their union. Mary of Scotland was dead, and the country was no longer distracted with divisions. All, Protestants and Catholics alike, were ready to gather round their Queen and do their utmost to keep out the foreigner. In the Royal Navy, when all was done, there were only thirty-four ships, with 6,279 men; but every nobleman and gentleman who was able, provided and

manned ships at his own expense, and the seaport towns sent out their vessels. In the end,
some 197 ships were got together, though many
of them were only small barques and pinnaces.
In number they exceeded the Spanish fleet, but
their tonnage only amounted to 30,144, whilst
that of the Armada was 59,120. In all his preparations, Lord Howard was aided by the advice
of the great English seamen, Drake, Hawkins, and
Frobisher. Drake was appointed Vice-Admiral,
and got together a fleet of sixty vessels at Plymouth. Most of these were volunteer barques
manned with the brave seamen of Devon and
Cornwall.

Meanwhile Sir Walter Ralegh was chiefly engaged in making preparations to defend the coast
and repel an invasion, should the Spaniards be
able to land. His advice seems to have been
much listened to in the Queen's councils. He
made large levies of the men of the Stannaries,
and did all he could to strengthen the defences of
the isle of Portland, of which he was governor.
At Tilbury an army was gathered together under
Leicester; and here Elizabeth, roused at last to
the sense of her danger, and full of courage to
meet it, tried to impart her own confidence to her
soldiers. "Let tyrants fear," she said. "I have
always so behaved myself that, under God, I have
placed my chiefest strength and safeguard in the
loyal hearts and good will of my subjects. . . . .
I know I have but the body of a weak and feeble

woman; but I have the heart of a king, and of a king of England too, and think it foul scorn that Parma, or Spain, or any prince of Europe, should dare to invade the borders of my realm; to which, rather than any dishonour should grow by me, I myself will take up arms, I myself will be your general, judge, and rewarder of every one of your virtues in the field."

The Invincible Armada left Lisbon towards the end of May. But the weather was against it, and the huge ships were unwieldy and difficult to manage. The commander, the Duke of Medina-Sidonia, was no great seaman, and his incompetence helped to delay the voyage. It was not till Friday, the 19th of July, that the Armada sighted the Lizard Point. The Spaniards hoped to surprise the English fleet; but they had been seen by a Cornish pirate, named Fleming. He put out all sail, and sped to Plymouth to give warning.

No time was lost in getting ready. The next morning Howard sailed out of Plymouth with sixty-seven vessels to await the coming of the Spaniards. Some of the fleet were off Dover, and vessels were scattered all along the south coast to keep watch. On the 20th of July, Howard saw the Spanish fleet pass by Plymouth. In obedience to the commands of Philip II. they were on their way to effect a meeting in the Channel with the Prince of Parma. Howard let them pass, and then pursued them, to attack and harass their rear. It would have been folly on the part of the English to risk a general engagement; but in chance skirmishes the swiftness with which their small, light vessels could move, gave them great advantages over the heavy galleons of the Spaniards. The little English ships, hanging on the rear of the mighty Armada, seized their opportunity, darted in amongst the unwieldy vessels, attacked and damaged them, and were gone before the Spaniards had time to retaliate.

The Spaniards, when they perceived the nimbleness of the enemy, arranged themselves in the form of a half moon, and slackened their sails, so that they might keep together, and that none of the ships might fall behind. When severely battered by the English shot, the Spanish ships gathered so close together for safety that one of the biggest galleons had her foremast damaged, and was left behind. This great ship, with four hundred and fifty men on board, fell into the hands of Drake, who treated his prisoners right honourably. He found also great treasure of gold in the ship.

The English fleet grew daily greater as it pursued the Armada, for ships and men came to join it out of all the harbours of England. They came "flocking as to a set field, where immortal fame and glory was to be attained, and faithful service to be performed unto their prince and country."

Sir Walter Ralegh joined the fleet on the 23rd July. He had probably been delayed on land by his preparations. Little is known of the part he played when with the fleet; but we cannot doubt that where all were brave he was amongst the bravest. Some, excited with the first successes of the English, advised Howard to grapple with the enemy's ships and board them. Referring to this in his *History of the World*, Ralegh says: "Charles Lord Howard, Admiral of England, would have been lost in the year 1588, if he had not been better advised than a great many malignant fools were that found fault with his behaviour. The Spaniards had an army aboard them, and he had none. They had more ships than he had, and of higher building and charging; so that had he entangled himself with those great and powerful vessels he had greatly endangered this kingdom of England; for twenty men upon the defence are equal to a hundred that board and enter. Whereas then, contrariwise, the Spaniards had an hundred for twenty of ours to defend themselves withal. But our Admiral knew his advantage, and held it, which had he not done, he had not been worthy to have held his head."

On the 24th July a council of the commanders was held, and the English fleet was divided into four squadrons, under Lord Howard, Sir Francis Drake, Captain Hawkins, and Captain Frobisher. On the 25th there was severe skirmishing off the Isle of Wight, in which Frobisher and Hawkins behaved themselves so valiantly, and withal so prudently, that on the following day the Lord Admiral rewarded them with the order of knighthood. As the two fleets passed through the Straits

of Calais, crowds of Frenchmen, Walloons, and
Flemings gathered on the coast of France to see
the wonderful sight. Never before in the history
of the world had such an array of ships been seen.
The Spanish fleet anchored off Calais; for the
Duke of Medina-Sidonia had received messengers,
telling him that Alexander of Parma would be
ready in a dozen hours or so to embark from
Dunkirk, and join him.

Meanwhile the English fleet had been joined by
twenty ships which had been keeping guard over
the mouth of the Thames. Howard now saw that
he could no longer avoid an engagement. If he
was to strike a decisive blow at the Spaniards, he
must do it before they were joined by Parma.
On the 28th of July, therefore, he took eight of
his worst and basest ships, and filled them with
gunpowder, pitch, brimstone, and other combus-
tibles, and setting them on fire, sent them, at
two o'clock in the morning, the wind and the
tide being favourable, into the midst of the Spanish
fleet. The Spaniards were roused from their sleep
in the dead of the night by these terrible burning
apparitions, and were thrown into such perplexity
and horror, that, cutting their cables and hoisting
their sails, they betook themselves very confusedly
into the main sea.

In the confusion the ships ran against one
another; and some were damaged by collision,
others were burnt by the fire-ships, and the remainder were driven northwards along the Flemish

coast by the wind and the tide. The English pursued them, and on July 29th there was a fierce battle fought off Gravelines. The attack was led by Drake, the Admiral not having yet come up. Again the English took advantage of their nimble steerage, and "came oftentimes very near upon the Spaniards, and charged them so sore that now and then they were but a pike's length asunder; and so continually giving them one broadside after another, they discharged all their shot, both great and small, upon them, . . . until such time as powder and bullets failed them." The fighting lasted six hours, and terrible mischief was done to the Spaniards. The Admiral Howard joined the battle before it was over; not a ship in the Spanish fleet escaped damage. "Their force is wonderful great and strong," wrote Howard; "but we pluck their feathers by little and little. . . Notwithstanding that our powder and shot was well near all spent, we set on a brag countenance, and gave them chase."

The wind came to the help of the English, and the Spaniards fled northwards with full sail. "There was never anything pleased me better," wrote Drake, "than seeing the enemy flying with a southerly wind northwards." For four days the English pursued; but on Friday, the 2nd of August, they had to halt, as powder and provisions were failing them. They left the winds and the waves to finish the work of destruction which they had begun. On the 4th of August, the

F

English fleet arrived at Harwich. There it provided itself with powder and provisions, and sailed out again to be ready to meet the Spanish fleet, should it return. But when the English heard that the Spaniards had determined to sail round the north of Scotland and Ireland, and so return home, "they thought it best to leave them unto those boisterous and uncouth northern seas, and not there to hunt after them." A terrible storm which arose on the 4th of August brought fearful sufferings to the Spanish ships. They were driven helplessly before the wind. Some were wrecked on the coasts of Norway; others were dashed to pieces on the Scottish shores; others only escaped to perish on the Irish coasts. In October the miserable remnant of the Invincible Armada reached Spain. Of that proud array of 132 ships, with 30,000 men, only fifty-three ships, with 10,000 men, returned. England had been delivered from terrible peril. It would be long before Philip II. could have another fleet on the seas; and meanwhile England had shown what stuff her mariners were made of, and made it clear that he would not find the task of crushing her an easy one. The defeat of the Armada showed the world that the power of Spain was declining, and that England was again able to fill an important position in the affairs of Europe.

CHAPTER VI

Ralegh in Disgrace.

A GLOOM was cast over Elizabeth's rejoicings at the defeat of the Armada by the death of the Earl of Leicester in the following September. A little while before his death Leicester, alarmed in all probability at the growing influence of Ralegh, had introduced a new favourite at Court, his stepson Robert Devereux, Earl of Essex. After Leicester's death, Essex held the chief place in the Queen's favour and at Court, and became the head of the party opposed to Ralegh.

Essex was young, only twenty-one years old, brave, handsome, full of generous feelings, but devoured by vanity and ambition. He rapidly made his way in the Queen's affections, and though more than thirty years his senior, she demanded from him all the devotion of a lover, and lavished upon him in return all the tenderness of a mistress.

It was hardly to be expected that Ralegh and Essex should get on well together. Ralegh felt himself supplanted by the new favourite, and his proud spirit could not put up with the slights cast

upon him by his rival, a mere upstart boy. He
withdrew from Court for a time, and went to visit
his estates in Ireland. Sir Francis Allen says, in
a letter written at this time, August, 1589, "My
Lord of Essex hath chased Mr. Ralegh from the
Court and hath confined him into Ireland."

In Ireland Ralegh either renewed an old friendship, or for the first time made friends, with
Edmund Spenser, the poet, then little known, who
was secretary to Lord Deputy Grey. In a poem,
dedicated to Ralegh, called "Colin Clouts come
home againe," Spenser thus describes Ralegh's
coming to Ireland:

> "One day (quoth he) I sat, (as was my trade)
>   Under the foot of Mole, that mountaine hore,
>   Keeping my sheepe amongst the cooly shade
>   Of the greene alders by the Mullaes shore:
>   There a straunge shepheard chaunst to find me out,
>   Whether allured with my pipes delight,
>   Whose pleasing sound yshrilled far about,
>   Or thither led by chaunce, I know not right:
>   Whom when I asked from what place he came,
>   And how he hight, himselfe he did ycleepe
>   The Shepheard of the Ocean by name,
>   And said he came far from the main-sea deepe.
>   He, sitting me beside in that same shade,
>   Provoked me to plaie some pleasant fit;
>   And, when he heard the musicke which I made,
>   He found himselfe full greatly pleasd at it:
>   Yet, æmuling my pipe, he tooke in hond
>   My pipe, before that æmuled of many,
>   And plaid thereon; (for well that skill he cond;*)
>   Himselfe as skilfull in that art as any.

---

* Knew.

He pip'd, I sung; and, when he sung, I piped;
By chaunge of turnes, each making other mery;
Neither envying other, nor envied,
So piped we, untill we both were weary."

Nothing could be more delightful than the description given by these lines of the way in which Ralegh and Spenser passed their time together. But they seem, besides making verses, to have talked of more serious things. When asked what the Shepherd of the Ocean sang about, Colin replies:

"His song was all a lamentable lay
Of great unkindnesse, and of usage hard,
Of Cynthia the Ladie of the Sea,
Which from her presence faultlesse him debard."

"Cynthia" was Queen Elizabeth; and from this we see that Ralegh complained of the harsh treatment he had received, which compelled him for a while to go away from Court. Colin then proceeds to tell how Ralegh persuaded him to

"Wend with him, his Cynthia to see,
Whose grace was great, and bounty most rewardfull."

Spenser returned to England with Ralegh in 1589, taking with him the three first books of the *Faerie Queen*. Ralegh must on his return soon have regained the Queen's favour; for he succeeded in getting for Spenser a kindly reception from the Queen. Spenser says—

"Yet found I lyking in her royall mynd,
Not for my skill, but for that shepheard's sake."

In 1590 Spenser published the three first books of the *Faerie Queen*, and Elizabeth granted him a

pension of £50 a year. Spenser prefixed to these
three books a letter to Ralegh, in which he set
forth the object of his work to be "to fashion a
gentleman or noble person in vertuous and gentle
discipline."

Though Ralegh managed to recover the place
in the Queen's favour which he had lost at first
through the jealousy of Essex, a love intrigue,
which the Queen chanced to discover, brought him
into still deeper disgrace. Amongst the fair ladies
at Queen Elizabeth's Court was one who made
a deeper impression upon the courtier's heart
than the royal mistress to whom he pretended
to make love. This was an orphan, Elizabeth
Throgmorton, one of Elizabeth's maids of honour,
a fair-haired, handsome woman, to whom Ralegh
made love secretly, probably afraid of the Queen's
anger, should she discover that he paid his devo-
tions to anyone but herself. Whilst Ralegh was
busy with his love affairs, he was also busy with
schemes for making reprisals on the Spaniards,
which occupied so many Englishmen after the
great Armada fight. Ralegh was probably anxious
to find some excuse for withdrawing from England
until the Queen's anger had blown over.

It was a splendid opportunity for gaining wealth
in the Spanish seas, and Elizabeth was more willing than ever to wink at the piracy of her subjects.
One of the most important of these enterprises
was undertaken by Lord Thomas Howard, cousin
of the Lord Admiral, and Sir Richard Grenville.

They set sail on the 10th March, 1591, with a fleet of some sixteen ships, to which Ralegh contributed one vessel. They hoped to seize a fleet bringing West Indian produce home to Spain; but Philip II. heard of their designs, and sent out a large fleet to oppose them. This fleet, consisting of fifty sail, was the biggest which the Spaniards had put on the sea since the Armada. Ralegh himself has left us an account of what followed, in a paper called, *The Truth of the Fight about the Isles of the Azores.*

The English fleet was riding at anchor off the Azores, on the afternoon of the last day of August, all unprepared to meet the enemy. "The ships," writes Ralegh, "all pestered and romaging, everything out of order. . . . The one-half part of the men of every ship sick and utterly unserviceable." The island had shrouded the approach of the Spanish fleet, and the English ships had scarce time to weigh their anchors. The last who got off was Sir Richard Grenville. He waited to take in the men who were on land, and who would otherwise have been lost. Howard managed to get away by the help of the wind, but Grenville could not do so. He then "utterly refused to turn from the enemy, alledging that he would rather choose to die than dishonour himself, his country, and Her Majesty's ship." So he turned with his single vessel to meet the Spanish fleet of fifty sail, hoping he might pass through the two squadrons in despite of them. Five Spanish ships attacked

the *Revenge*. They made divers attempts to enter
her, "but were repulsed again and again, and at
all times beaten back into their own ships or into
the seas. The fight began at three o'clock in the
afternoon, and continued very terrible all that
evening. The Spanish ships which attempted to
board the *Revenge*, as they were wounded and
beaten off, so always others came in their places;
she having never less than two mighty galleons
by her sides." So it went on all through the
night ; but as the day increased so the men of the
Revenge decreased. At last "all the powder of the
Revenge to the last barrel was spent, all her pikes
broken, forty of her best men slain, and the most
part of the rest hurt." Unto them "remained no
comfort at all; no hope, no supply either of ships,
men, or weapons. . . . The masts all beaten over-
board; all her tackle cut asunder. . . . Sir Richard,
finding himself in this distress, having endured in
this fifteen hours' fight the assault of fifteen several
armadas, . . . commanded the master gunner to
split and sink the ship." He was determined to
die rather than surrender to his enemies. The
master gunner felt as he did ; but the other officers
begged Sir Richard to have care of them. When
he would not hearken to them, they took the
matter into their own hands, and treated with the
Spanish Admiral, Alfonzo Bazan, who gave them
honourable terms; for he granted "that all their
lives should be saved, the company sent for England, and the better sort to pay such reasonable

ransome as their estate would bear, and in the
mean season to be free from galley or imprisonment. . . . Sir Richard, being thus overmatched,
was sent unto by Alfonzo Bazan, to remove out of
the *Revenge*, the ship being marvellous unsavoury,
filled with blood, and bodies of dead and wounded
men, like a slaughter-house. Sir Richard answered
that he might do with his body what he list; for he
esteemed it not; and as he was carried out of the
ship he swooned, and reviving again, desired the
company to pray for him." The Spaniards, who
greatly respected him for his valour, tended him
with the utmost care; but he died of his wounds
the second or third day after he had been taken
on board the Spanish ship. "Here die I," he said
to the Spaniards who stood round, "Richard Grenville, with a joyfull and quiet mind, for that I
have ended my life as a good soldier ought to do,
who has fought for his country and his Queen, for
honour and religion. Wherefore my soul joyfully
departeth out of this body, leaving behind it an
everlasting fame, as a true soldier who hath done
his duty as he was bound to do. But the others
of my company have done as traitors and dogs;
for which they shall be reproached all their lives,
and have a shameful name for ever." Grenville's
condemnation does not seem to have been deserved
by Lord Thomas Howard, who would have come
to his assistance, if his crews would have let him.
Ralegh thinks it was better that he did not, considering the smallness of his fleet, its bad condition,

and the sickness of the men. "The dishonour and loss to the Queen had been far greater than the spoil or harm that the enemy could any way have received."

After this fight a tremendous storm arose, and did great havoc amongst the Spanish fleet; and also to the fleet of Spanish treasure-ships coming home from the West Indies. "Thus," adds Ralegh, "it hath pleased God to fight for us, and to defend the justice of our cause against the ambitious and bloody pretences of the Spaniards, who, seeking to devour all nations, are themselves devoured." Ralegh looked upon ceaseless opposition to the Spaniard as the sacred duty of every Englishman. He seems to have grasped the nature of Philip II.'s vast schemes to restore the Romish faith, and place puppet kings on the thrones of France and Germany. With a monarch who cherished such schemes there could be no possibility of peace; and it was this feeling, as much as love of booty, that sent the English privateers into the Spanish seas. Grenville's fight in the *Revenge* shows the spirit which animated them. They knew no fear, they counted no costs before they attacked, but trusted to their own courage and to God. Doubtless the rich booty won in these fights was very welcome; but a larger motive existed besides the love of plunder, and in some perhaps was the strongest. "Let not any Englishman," writes Ralegh, "of what religion soever, have other opinion of the Spaniard, but . . . that he useth

his pretence of religion for no other purpose but
to bewitch us from the obedience of our natural
Prince, thereby hoping in time to bring us to
slavery and subjection." As Ralegh grew older,
and learned more, his opposition to Spain grew
more and more statesmanlike. With this view
he wished to found colonies, that through them
England's trade and wealth might grow, and she
might become more able to resist the encroachments of Spain.

In 1592 Ralegh planned a new attack upon
Spain. The Queen lent him two ships, and he
fitted out thirteen others. With these he intended
to sail towards the Isthmus of Darien, and lie in
wait there for Spanish treasure-ships. This time
he started himself with the fleet on the 6th of May,
1592. But the next day he was overtaken by a
swift pinnace, in which was Sir Martin Frobisher,
bearing a letter from Elizabeth bidding him return
at once.

On the 11th of May accordingly he left the fleet,
giving one squadron in charge to Frobisher, and
another to Sir John Burroughs. There is some
obscurity about the cause of Ralegh's recall. It
is generally supposed that Queen Elizabeth had
found out his intrigue with Bessy Throgmorton,
and wished to punish him for it. It is supposed
by others that she did not like her favourite to
run any risk, and that this recall had been arranged with himself before he started. Be this
as it may, his love affair was known to the Queen

immediately after his return, and in July, 1592, Ralegh was lodged in the Tower for his offence.

Two years before, Essex had excited the Queen's bitter anger by his marriage with Frances Walsingham, the widow of Sir Philip Sidney. So violent was Elizabeth's anger, that in a letter written from Court, even some months after, we find it said : "The earl doth use it with good temper, concealing his marriage as much as so open a matter may be; not that he denies it to any, but, for her Majesty's better satisfaction, is pleased that my lady should live very retired in her mother's house." But Elizabeth could not get on without Essex, and her love for him was strong enough to make her overlook his marriage, and receive him into favour again.

With Ralegh it was different. In her first burst of anger Elizabeth committed him to the Tower. His enemies did their utmost to keep him in disgrace, so that he remained under the cloud of royal displeasure for a long while, and never quite regained his former favour. It is not possible to fix the date of his marriage with Elizabeth Throgmorton ; but it seems to have taken place some time in 1592, whether before or after his imprisonment we do not know.

From the Tower Ralegh wrote letters describing, in the exaggerated language of the time, his despair at being banished from the presence of his royal mistress. In a letter written in July, 1592, he describes himself as "being become like a fish

cast on dry land gasping for breath, with lame
legs and lamer lungs." In another letter written
to Sir Robert Cecil, Burleigh's son, in July, 1592,
when Elizabeth was just starting on a progress, he
says: "My heart was never broken till this day
that I hear the Queen goes so far off, whom I have
followed so many years with so great love and
desire in so many journeys, and am now left behind her, in a dark prison all alone. While she
was yet nigh at hand, that I might hear of her
once in two or three days, my sorrows were the
less: but even now my heart is cast into the
depth of all misery. I that was wont to behold
her riding like Alexander, hunting like Diana,
walking like Venus, the gentle wind blowing her
fair hair about her pure cheeks like a nymph,
sometime sitting in the shade like a goddess,
sometime singing like an angel, sometime play-
ing like an Orpheus." He ends his letter by
saying, "Do with me as you list; I am more
weary of life than they are desirous I should
perish." When we think that Ralegh was writing
of a woman in her sixtieth year, this language
seems absurdly overstrained; but such was the
fashion of the day.

One day Ralegh saw from the windows of the
Tower the Queen in her barge, followed by a
gay procession of boats, pass down the river.
"Suddenly," we are told by Sir Arthur Gorges,
who was present, "he brake out into a great distemper, and swore that his enemies had brought

her Majesty thither to break his gall in sunder
with Tantalus torment; that when she went away
he might see his death before his eyes." He swore
that he would disguise himself and get a sight of
the Queen, or "his heart would break." As his
keeper, Sir George Carew, would not consent, a
quarrel followed, in which they ended by drawing
their daggers. Gorges thus describes the scene to
Cecil: "At the first I was ready to break with
laughing, to see the two scramble and brawl like
madmen, until I saw the iron walking, and then
I did my best to appease the fury. As yet I
cannot reconcile them by any persuasions; for Sir
Walter swears that he shall hate him while he
lives, for so restraining him from a sight of his
mistress." Gorges ends his letter by saying that
he fears Sir Walter Ralegh "will shortly grow to be
Orlando Furioso if the bright Angelica persevere
against him a little longer."

Whilst Ralegh was still in the Tower, news
arrived that the portion of the fleet which he
had despatched under Burroughs had captured a
splendid prize, a large Spanish carrack, of 1,600
tons burden, called *La Madre de Dios*. It was
laden with spices, drugs, silks, calicos, quilts,
carpets, and colours, to the value of £150,000.
This rich prize was brought home to Dartmouth.
Of course the sailors had managed to pillage
something before Burroughs was able to take formal
possession of the ship in her Majesty's name. It
now remained to divide the spoil amongst those

who had shared the expenses of the enterprise; the chief of these were the Queen, the Earl of Cumberland, and Ralegh himself. Elizabeth did not disdain to share, as a private person, in the expense of fitting out an expedition having no other aim than piracy, and she was content to enrich herself with the spoil.

The news of the great prize filled the country with excitement. Merchants hurried to Dartmouth in the hope of making good bargains with the sailors for the plunder they had managed to secure. The port is said to have looked like "Bartholomew fair." The Queen appointed commissioners to go down to look after her interest in the capture, the chief of whom was Sir Robert Cecil. She also allowed Ralegh to go down to look after his interests, though she sent a keeper with him to see that he did not escape. The excitement on the arrival of the *Madre de Dios* caused great confusion. The sailors were mutinous from their desire to lay hands on the booty, and it was absolutely necessary that some commanding spirit should be there to keep order. "To bring this to some good effect," wrote Sir John Hawkins, "Sir Walter Ralegh is the very man."

Sir Robert Cecil was very anxious to reach Dartmouth before Ralegh; and in an amusing letter to his father, Lord Burleigh, he gives an account of his journey. "Whomsoever I met by the way," he writes, "within seven miles, with anything either in cloke or malle which did but

smell of the prizes, either at Dartmouth or at
Plymouth, for I assure your lordship I could
smell them, such hath been the spoils of amber
and musk, I did, though he had little about him,
return him with me to the town of Exeter. . . . .
I compelled them also to tell me where any
malles or trunks were, and I by this inquisition—
finding the people stubborn till I had committed
two of them to prison, which example would have
won the Queen £20,000 a week past—I have
lighted upon a Londoner, in whose possession we
have found a bag of seed pearls, divers pieces of
damask, &c. I do mean, my lord, forthwith to be
at Dartmouth, and to have a privy search there
and in Plymouth. . . . . I have taken order to
search every bag and mail coming from the west;
and though I fear that the bird be flown for jewels,
pearls, and amber, yet I will not doubt to save
her Majesty . . . that which shall be worth my
journey. My lord, there was never such spoil. . . .
And thus in haste I humbly take my leave from
Exeter, ready to ride to Dartmouth this night at
ten of the clock. I will suppress the confluence
of these buyers, of which there are above two
thousand; and except they be removed there
will be no good. The name of commissioners is
common in this country and in these causes; but
my coming down hath made many stagger. Fouler
weather, desperate ways, nor more obstinate people
did I never meet with."

From Dartmouth Cecil writes again: "As soon

as I came on board the carrack on Wednesday, at
one of the clock, with the rest of her Majesty's
commissioners, within one hour Sir Walter Ralegh
arrived with his keeper, Mr. Blount. I assure you,
sir, his poor servants, to the number of a hundred
and forty goodly men, and all the mariners, came
to him with shouts of joy, as I never saw a man
more troubled to quiet them in my life. But his
heart is broken, for he is extremely pensive, longer
than he is busied, in which he can toil terribly;
but if you did hear him rage at the spoils, finding
all the short wares utterly devoured, you would
laugh as I do, which I cannot choose. . . . . He
belike finding that it is known he had a keeper,
whensoever he is saluted with congratulations
for liberty, he doth answer, 'No; I am still the
Queen of England's poor captive.' I wished him
to conceal it, because here it doth diminish his
credit, which I do vow to you before God is
greater amongst the mariners than I thought for.
I do grace him as much as I may; for I find him
marvellously greedy to do anything to recover the
conceit of his brutish offence."

From this letter, written by an opponent of
Ralegh's, we can judge of his popularity amongst
the men of his own county. Ralegh was not, as a
rule, a popular man. His manners were haughty
and overbearing; but in Devonshire, and amongst
sailors, he seems to have succeeded in winning
universal love.

The spoil of the *Madre de Dios* was divided

G

with some difficulty, and a good deal of squab-
bling. Elizabeth's greedy spirit showed itself in
her desire to get as much as possible at all costs
for herself. Ralegh was very anxious to recover
some of the jewels which had been stolen from
the ship. He wrote to Burleigh, on September
17th : "If it please your lordship to send a commission to Alderman Marten and others, to make
inquiry into London what goldsmiths or jewellers
are gone down, and that at their return they may
be examined upon oath what stones or pearls they
have bought, I doubt not but many things will be
discovered. If I meet any of them coming up, if
it be upon the wildest heath in all the way, I
mean to strip them as naked as ever they were
born ; for it is infinite that her Majesty hath been
robbed, and that of the most rare things."

The Queen of course got the best part of the
profits. She took somewhat more than half of the
net proceeds. The Earl of Cumberland got £36,000,
having adventured in the enterprize £19,000. The
rest of the adventurers, whose share in the expense
of the expedition amounted to £30,000, only got
£36,000 ; and Ralegh, after summing up the services that he had rendered the expedition, adds
bitterly, that "the others only sat still, for which
double is given to them, and less than mine own
to me."

There is something very undignified in the
spectacle of the Queen and her courtiers quarrelling for the plunder won from Spain by piracy.

Elizabeth wished in every way to make the most of her bargain. The sale of certain precious articles was forbidden in the ordinary way of trade, so as to get a better market for the merchandise from the *Madre de Dios;* so that the prize was probably not of so much benefit to the people as to their Queen.

CHAPTER VII.

Ralegh's First Voyage to Guiana

AFTER his journey to Dartmouth Ralegh did
not go back to the Tower; though it is un-
certain when he was relieved of the company of
his keeper. He was not again received into favour
at Court, or allowed for some years to exercise his
duties as Captain of the Guard. In May, 1593,
we find him at Sherborne Castle.

This manor of Sherborne, which lay upon the
road between London and Plymouth, had attracted
Sir Walter's admiration as he passed it on his
frequent journeys to Devon and Cornwall. It
belonged to the bishopric of Salisbury, which had
once been seated at Sherborne. When Ralegh cast
longing eyes upon it, the Queen, who was not
scrupulous about the way in which she deprived
the church of its lands, made the bishop give
her a lease of ninety-nine years of the estate,
which she made over to her favourite. Ralegh
wished to get absolute possession of the estate.
When the see of Salisbury next fell vacant, it
was decided to make the gift of it conditional on a

promise from the new bishop that he would convey
over to the Queen, for the benefit of Ralegh, the
estate of Sherborne. The first man to whom the
see was offered on these terms refused it; but it
was accepted by Dr. Henry Cotton, Prebendary of
Winchester, in 1598, and the estate of Sherborne
was granted to Ralegh. In return, an annuity of
£260 was granted to the see of Salisbury in perpetuity. From this and suchlike proceedings of
Elizabeth towards the church, we may see that
the royal supremacy was in its way as oppressive
to the clergy as the pope's supremacy had been.

Ralegh made Sherborne his chief residence, and
did much to improve it. He shared the taste of
the age for building and gardening. A great improvement was made in those days in the homes
of the gentry. The days of civil war were past
and forgotten. The fortified castles of former times
were no longer needed. Men wanted comfort
for their daily life, and a new style of domestic
architecture sprung up, which has since borne
the name of Elizabethan architecture. It was a
combination of the old Gothic with classical
architecture, the taste for which had been called
out by the revival of classical learning, and it
was admirably fitted for domestic purposes. The
comfort of the houses inside was also greatly increased. The walls were covered with tapestry,
or wainscoted with oak. Feather-beds were in
common use. Stoves began to be used in the
houses of the gentry; cupboards full of silver

adorned the walls; china dishes and plates and rare Venetian glass were favourite articles of luxury. We read in the *Dorsetshire County History* that Ralegh first began to build on to the castle at Sherborne " very fairly; but altering his purpose, he built in the park adjoining a most fine house, which he beautified with orchards, gardens, and groves of much variety and great delight; so that whether you consider the pleasantness of the seat, the goodness of the soil, or the other delicacies belonging to it, it rests unparalleled by any in that part of the country." In his present retirement at Sherborne he probably enjoyed the society of his wife, and the amusement of planning and laying out his gardens. But he was not a man to delight in leisure. Shut out for a time from any chance of gaining power or influence at Court or in the government, his busy mind turned to other schemes.

The wealth which Spain was believed to gain from her colonies and conquests in South America filled the English with envy. They saw their own country poor, their Queen obliged to be parsimonious, unable to engage in war from the want of the necessary money. To enrich England by founding colonies was, as we have seen, Ralegh's dream. The stories of the conquests of Peru and Mexico by Pizarro and Cortez had filled Europe with wonder and admiration. To gain a like rich kingdom for his Queen, to fill her exchequer, to extend her power, was Ralegh's ambition. But he wished to do it in a different way from the Spaniards. He did not wish to imitate their cruelty to the natives. Instead of making the natives bitter enemies, he wished to make them friends; to bring their kings to seek the alliance and protection of England; and by gaining a mighty subject kingdom for Elizabeth, to set her resources on a level with those which the Spanish King was supposed to have.

With these thoughts in his mind, Ralegh turned his attention to Guiana. He seems to have laid aside his plans for colonizing Virginia, being dazzled by the wondrous tales that he heard about Guiana. Since the early days of Spanish discovery in America, the natives had poured into the ears of the eager and wondering foreigners tales of the untold wealth of Guiana, the country that lay round the great river Orinoco. Fables of the vast city of Manoa and of El Dorado passed from mouth to mouth. The name of El Dorado was first given to the King of this wondrous city, afterwards to the city itself. The empire of Guiana had greater abundance of gold than any part of Peru. Manoa, for greatness, riches, and its excellent situation, far surpassed any city in the world. To this city it was supposed that all the treasure which had been saved from the hands of the Spaniards at the time of the conquests of Mexico and Peru had been carried. Gold was thought to be so plentiful there that " the very boxes and troughs were made of gold

and silver, and billets of gold lay about in heaps."
The men of the country were said to adorn their
bodies by powdering them with gold.

The Spaniards had spared no pains to explore
and gain possession of this land of promise. Between 1530 and 1560 seven or eight Spanish
expeditions had attempted to penetrate into it;
but the expeditions were unfortunate, and thou-
sands of Spaniards perished in the attempt.
Ralegh hoped to succeed where they had failed;
and he hoped to succeed, not by conquering the
natives, but by making friends of them. In
Guiana he could best find the wealth which England needed; and in no way could he better aim
a blow at Spain than by snatching from her the
rich prize which she so coveted.

So, in retirement at Sherborne, Ralegh planned
his first expedition to Guiana. It was a splendid
dream for a private individual to cherish, and its
difficulties did not daunt Ralegh. His wife however was terrified at the thought of the danger
which he might run, and she wrote to Sir Robert
Cecil, whom she looked upon as a firm friend,
begging him to dissuade Ralegh from his undertaking. "Now, sir," she wrote, in February, 1593,
"for the rest I hope, for my sake, you will rather
draw *water* (Sir Walter Ralegh) from the east than
help him towards the sunset, if any respect to me
or love to him be not forgotten. . . . . We poor
souls that have bought sorrow at a high price, desire, and can be pleased with, the same misfortunes

that we hold, fearing alterations will but multiply miseries." But Ralegh was not to be dissuaded. Neither indeed was Cecil very anxious to dissuade him; for he himself contributed to the expense of fitting out the expedition. The Lord High Admiral Howard lent a ship, and numbers of gentlemen volunteered on the expedition.

In 1594 Ralegh sent Captain Whiddon as a pioneer to explore the mouths of the river Orinoco. But Whiddon learnt little that was new, having met with many difficulties, and returned to England towards the end of the year. Ralegh was now busy with preparations for his own voyage, and on the 6th February, 1595, he sailed from Plymouth with a squadron of five ships. He has himself written an account of his voyage, so that we are able accurately to follow his steps. He reached the island of Trinidad on the 22nd of March. Coasting round it, he came to Puerto de los Espannoles, where some Spaniards came on board to trade with the crew, "all which," he says, "I entertained kindly and feasted after our manner, by means whereof I learnt of one and another as much of the estate of Guiana as I could." Ralegh was anxious to make himself master of Trinidad before going further; had he not done so, he says, "he would have savoured very much of the ass." He took the Spanish city of St. Joseph, and made its governor, Don Antonio Berreo, prisoner. He then did his utmost to make friends with the Indians on the island, telling them that he was the servant of a Queen who was an enemy of the Spaniards "in respect of their tyranny and oppression, and that she delivered all such nations about her as were by them oppressed." The result of his discourse was, that "in that part of the world her Majesty is now very famous and admirable."

The first difficulty which met the adventurers was the navigation of the mouths of the Orinoco. On account of the sandbanks and the shifting tides, it was impossible for the ships to go up the mouth of the river. So Ralegh had to decide to leave his ships anchored on the coast of Trinidad, near Los Gallos, and proceed on his expedition in five open boats, which carried one hundred men and enough provisions for a month. "First of all," writes Ralegh, "we had as much sea to cross over in our wherries as between Dover and Calais, and in a great billow, the wind and current being both very strong." They took with them an Indian as pilot, who promised to bring them into the great river Orinoco, "but indeed of that which he entered he was utterly ignorant; for he had not seen it in twelve years before, at which time he was very young and of no judgement, and if God had not sent us another help we might have wandered a whole year in that labyrinth of rivers. . . . For I know all the earth doth not yield a like confluence of streams and branches, the one crossing the other so many times, and all so fair and large and so like one

another, as no man can tell which to take." The
good chance which befell Ralegh was the capture
of an old Indian who really knew the country,
and who was able to act as their pilot through
the sixteen arms which the Orinoco makes where
it falls into the sea. The next difficulty which
beset the adventurers was the rapidity of the
current. After rowing four days through the
intricate branchings of the river "we fell," says
Ralegh, "into as goodly a river as ever I beheld,
called the great Amana, which ran more directly
without windings or turnings than the other; but
soon the flood of the sea left us, and being enforced either by main strength to row against a
violent current, or to return as wise as we went,
we had then no shift but to persuade the companies that it was but two or three days' work,
and therefore desired them to take pains, every
gentleman and others taking their turns to row.
When three days more were overgone, our companies began to despair, the weather being ex-
treme hot, the river bordered with very high
trees that kept away the air, and the current
against us every day stronger than the other;
but we evermore commanded our pilots to promise an end the next day, and used it so long
as we were driven to assure them from four
reaches of the river to three, and so to two, and
so to the next reach; but so long we laboured
that many days were spent, and we driven to
draw ourselves to harder allowance, our bread

even at the last, and no drink at all, and our men and ourselves so wearied and scorched, and doubtful withall whether we should ever perform it or no, the heat increasing as we drew near the line; for we were now in five degrees."

The variety of the scenery did something towards cheering them on their way. "On the banks of these rivers were divers sorts of fruits good to eat, flowers and trees of such variety as were sufficient to make ten volumes of herbals. We relieved ourselves many times with the fruits of the country, and sometimes with fowl and fish. We saw birds of all colours—some carnation, some crimson, orange-tawney, purple, &c.; and it was unto us a great good passing time to behold them, besides the relief we found by killing some store of them with our fowling-pieces." At last the Indian pilot led Ralegh and a few others some way up a branch stream to an Indian village, where they were hospitably received, and got good store of bread, fish, and hens. To reach this village they passed through most beautiful country, plains twenty miles long, with the grass short and green, where the deer came down feeding by the waterside.

After Ralegh returned to the rest of the company they had the good fortune to take two canoes, which they found laden with bread. This excellent bread so delighted the men that they cried, "Let us go on, we care not how far." Two other canoes escaped their pursuit, one of which they heard contained three Spaniards. On the bank they found hidden under a bush a refiner's basket, with divers things needful for the trial of metals. They heard that the three Spaniards had a good quantity of ore and gold with them. They tried hard to catch them, but in vain. They laid hands however on an Indian who had served as pilot to the Spaniards, and gave Ralegh much information about the gold mines.

The Spaniards had told the Indians that the English were men-eaters, hoping by this tale to keep them from having any intercourse with the English. But Ralegh compelled his men to treat the Indians so well, that they soon perceived the falseness of the Spaniards' tales, and felt great love for the strangers. " But I confess," writes Ralegh, " it was a very impatient work to keep the meaner sort from spoil and stealing when we came to their houses; which because in all I could not prevent, I caused my Indian interpreter at every place when we departed to know of the loss or wrong done; and if aught were stolen or taken by violence, either the same was restored, and the offender punished, or else was paid for to their uttermost demand." The result of this treatment was that the Indians came down in crowds to the water-banks with their women and children to gaze at the wonderful strangers, and bring them food, venison, pork, fowls, fish, excellent fruits, and roots; above all, the pine-apple, " that prince of fruits," as Ralegh calls it.

The English were hospitably received at the little towns, some of which were well-situated and surrounded with goodly gardens. In one of these towns Ralegh had much talk with an old chief, called Topiawari, who "is held for the proudest and wisest of all the Orenoqueponi, and so behaved himself, as I marvelled to find a man of that gravity and judgment, and of so good discourse, that had no help of learning or breed." Topiawari told Ralegh much about the different peoples of that country, and promised to come and see him again on his way back.

The onward progress of the travellers was soon stopped by the rapid rise of the rivers, caused by the first heavy winter rains. They halted at the beginning of a river called Caroli, and three parties went out to explore the country by land. Ralegh with another party went to see some wonderful falls formed by the river Caroli: "a strange thunder of waters," he calls them. "Never saw I a more beautifull country nor more lively prospects—hills so raised here and there over the valleys, the river winding into divers branches, the plains all fair green grass, the deer crossing in every path, the birds towards evening singing on every tree with a thousand several tunes, the air fresh with a gentle easterly wind, and every stone that we stooped to take up promised either gold or silver by its complexion." The other companies brought back equally favourable reports; but it seemed high time to return,

for "the river began to rage and to overflow very
fearfully, and the rains came down in terrible
showers and gusts in great abundance, and withal
our men began to cry out for want of shift; for
no man had place to bestow any other apparel
than that which he wore on his back, and that
was thoroughly washt on his body for the most
part ten times in one day."

On his way back Ralegh sent for old Topiawari,
to have some more talk with him. He came at
once, and with him "such a rabble of all sorts of
people, and everyone laden with somewhat, as if
it had been a great market or fair in England;
and our hungry companies clustered thick and
threefold among their baskets, everyone laying
hand on what he wanted." Ralegh took Topiawari
to his tent, and shut out everyone but his interpreter; then he asked Topiawari's advice as to
the means to be employed for conquering Guiana.
Topiawari bade him not attempt to invade the
strong parts of Guiana without the help of the
nations around, who were enemies of the great
Emperor Inga, who ruled in Guiana. Ralegh's
force was not strong enough to attempt the conquest now; and besides, the winter season was
unfavourable; and Topiawari, for these and other
reasons, strongly persuaded him to do nothing
further at present, but to come again the following
year. The old Indian chieftain freely gave Ralegh
his only son to take with him to England, hoping
that under the protection of the English he would

rule his land after his death. Ralegh left two
Englishmen behind with Topiawari to learn the
language.

On his way back Ralegh spent some time in
exploring different parts of the river, gaining
information from the natives, and collecting
specimens of ore to take back to England with
him. He sent off six men under Captain Keymis
to explore part of the country on foot, and meanwhile went himself some way up a branch of the
river called the Piacoa. He returned again to
meet Keymis, and they set off in haste to get
back to their ships; for their "hearts were cold to
behold the great rage and increase of the Orinoco."
The weather was very stormy, and the current
so strong that they went a hundred miles a day.
At the mouth of the river they were overtaken by
a mighty storm; but it was not safe to anchor
there, and so they trusted themselves to God's
keeping, and thrust out into the sea to cross to
Trinidad, "being all very sober and melancholy,
one faintly cheering another to show courage."
They reached the coast of Trinidad in safety, and
found their ships at anchor, "than which there
was never to us a more joyfull sight."

Ralegh reached England some time in August,
1595. He came home deeply convinced of the
wealth and glory that might be gained in Guiana.
"The common soldier," he writes, "shall here fight
for gold. Those commanders and chieftains that
shoot at honour and abundance shall find there

more rich and beautifull cities, more temples
adorned with golden images, more sepulchres
filled with treasure, than either Cortez found in
Mexico, or Pezarro in Peru; and the shining glory
of this conquest will eclipse all those so far ex-
tended beams of the Spanish nation." But his
enthusiasm failed to inspire others in England.
He was still out of favour at Court; he had many
enemies, and their jealousy went so far that some
said he had never been to Guiana at all, but had
remained hidden in Cornwall. Others asserted
that the ore which he had brought home had been
found, not in Guiana, but in Barbary, and carried
thence to Guiana. It was these calumnies which
led him to write and publish his account of this
voyage to Guiana, which was widely read, and
passed through two editions in the first year.

People were interested; but the nation was
not stirred to make any great effort to win this
rich prize. The Queen was too old to throw
herself with enthusiasm into so great a scheme.
Ralegh's unpopularity prevented men from gather-
ing round him, and aiding him with all their
might to carry out his plans. Still, without
doubt, the story of this voyage produced a great
effect. The description of these new and beau-
teous lands stirred men's imaginations in a way
which we can best see in the works of England's
greatest poet.

It is most likely that Ralegh, who we know
was on intimate terms with Ben Jonson, knew

H

Shakspeare too; and probably from his own lips
Shakspeare heard the story of his voyage. He
seems to have been thinking of Ralegh's travels,
and of the strange tales he had brought home,
when he makes Othello say:

> " Wherein I spoke of most disastrous chances;
>   Of moving accidents by flood and field; . . .
>   And portance in my traveller's history,
>   (Wherein of antres vast, and deserts idle,
>   Rough quarries, rocks, and hills whose heads touch heaven,
>   It was my hint to speak,) such was my process;—
>   And of the Cannibals that each other eat,
>   The Anthropophagi, and men whose heads
>   Do grow beneath their shoulders."

Ralegh's account of his voyage is full of tales
that he had heard of strange races of men; above
all, of the race who were said to have their eyes
in their shoulders, and their mouths in the middle
of their breasts.

But the *Tempest* seems most of all to have
been inspired by the tales of adventure which
passed from mouth to mouth in those days. In
this play Shakspeare shows us, in Caliban, the
savage whose peace was disturbed, and whose
haunts were invaded by the colonist and the ex-
plorer. He felt the pathos of the situation, and
can awaken our sympathy even with the brutal
Caliban when he says:

> " When thou camest first,
> Thou strok'dst me, and mad'st much of me; would'st give me
> Water with berries in 't; and teach me how
> To name the bigger light, and how the less,

That burn by day and night: and then I lov'd thee,
And show'd thee all the qualities o' the isle,
The fresh springs, brine-pits, barren place, and fertile;
Cursed be I that did so!"

The views of the majority of colonists and explorers are expressed in Prospero's remark to
Caliban:

" But thy vile race
Though thou didst learn, had that in 't which good natures
Could not abide to be with."

The savage was far more ready to learn the evil
than the good.   Caliban exclaims:

" You taught me language; and my profit on 't
Is, I know how to curse."

To the savage the greater knowledge and capacity
of the European appeared like magic; and so
Shakspeare has represented Prospero as ruling in
the island over winds and waves, and subduing
Caliban by his arts as a sorcerer.

Though Ralegh failed to inspire others with his
views about Guiana, he did not on that account
lose heart.   About six months after his return he
sent off, at his own expense, Captain Lawrence
Keymis in a ship to explore the Orinoco further.
Keymis was as enthusiastic as Ralegh himself
about the prospects of exploration in Guiana, and
says himself that he meant to devote his life to
it.   In this voyage, however, he failed to do
much.   The Spaniards, alarmed at Ralegh's proceedings, had done their utmost to forestall him;
and Keymis heard from the Indians that a Spanish

settlement, called St. Thome, had been made near Caroli with a special view of defending the passage to the mines, whence Ralegh had got his specimens of ore.

The Indians on all sides entreated Keymis to turn out the Spaniards; they welcomed the English warmly, and seemed to have awaited their return with impatience. Keymis had repeatedly to assure them that he had come only to trade, and had not brought a force sufficient to do anything against the Spaniards. He explored some new portions of the river, and returned to England in the same year. Ralegh sent out still another expedition before the year was over under Captain Berry, which however did nothing important. But we shall see that Ralegh never lost sight of his projects of colonization in Guiana. He was so firmly convinced of the great results that might be gained from it, that he was ready to seize every opportunity to carry out the schemes which seemed to have become part of himself.

CHAPTER VIII.

The Attack on Cadiz.

RALEGH was not received again into favour at Court on his return from Guiana, and was not allowed to go back to his duties as Captain of the Queen's Guard. But we are told in a contemporary letter that "he lived about town very gallant," and he seems to have been on good terms with the chief men about Court. "He was very often very private with the Earl of Essex," and did his utmost to bring about a better understanding between him and Sir Robert Cecil, Burleigh's son, who by his diligence and careful attention to politics was rapidly becoming an important person in the state, and who greatly resented Essex's influence.

Meanwhile, every one was terrified by the increasing power of Spain. In the beginning of 1596 the Spanish forces had managed to seize Calais, and by so doing had filled the English and Netherlanders with alarm. There was again fear of a Spanish invasion of England; but this time the English determined to be beforehand with Philip II. A fleet was equipped, which, in combination with a Dutch fleet, was to attack the harbour of Cadiz. This expedition was talked of for a long time. Essex and Ralegh were eager for it. The Queen and Burleigh, always lovers of peace, had in their old age grown more than ever opposed to war. But at last it became clear that something must be done to stop the growth of Philip's power, and active preparations for the expedition were begun. Drake and Hawkins had both lately died; but there were still plenty of brave seamen to fight for their country. It was arranged that the Lord Admiral Howard should command the fleet, whilst Essex was to command the land forces embarked for the expedition. Ralegh, who was extremely active in the preparations, was to have command of a squadron. Great difficulties were experienced in getting levies of men for the fleet. Ralegh writes to Cecil: "As fast as we press men one day, they come away another, and say they will not serve; and the poursuivant found me in a country village a mile from Gravesend, hunting after runaway mariners, and dragging in the mire from alehouse to alehouse."

At last everything was ready, and on the 3rd of June, 1596, the fleet set sail from Plymouth, and reached Cadiz on the 20th of the same month. As they waited outside the harbour in a high wind, "there lighted a very fair dove upon the mainyard of the Lord Admiral's ship, and there she sat very quietly for the space of three or four

hours, being nothing dismayed all the while."
To most of the men this appeared in the light
of a good omen to cheer them on their way.

In the harbour of Cadiz was a splendid Spanish
fleet, consisting of four huge galleons, between
twenty and thirty war-ships, and fifty-seven
well-armed Indiamen. In the allied fleet were
thirty-three English ships of war, and twenty-
seven Dutch, besides some transports. Essex's
desire was to land his soldiers, and begin an
attack on the town before attacking the fleet in
the bay; and the Lord Admiral, from his care of
the Queen's ships, had agreed to this. "Myself,"
writes Ralegh, "was not present at the resolution,
for I had been sent the day before to stop such
as might pass out along the coast. When I was
arrived back again I found the Earl of Essex
disembarking his soldiers, and he had put many
companies into boats. . . . The Earl purposed to
go on, until such time as I came aboard him,
and in the presence of all the colonels protested
against the resolution, giving him reasons and
making apparent demonstrations that he therebye
ran the way of our general ruin, to the utter overthrow of the whole armies, their own lives, and
her Majesty's future safety." The other gentlemen present warmly seconded Ralegh, and his
wisdom prevailed. He persuaded the Admiral to
attack the fleet first; and when he told Essex of
this resolution, the Earl cast his plumed hat into
the sea for joy.

Ralegh's advice seems to have been listened to in everything. At his earnest entreaty, the charge of leading the body of the fleet was entrusted to him. The attack began the next morning. The mark which Ralegh shot at was the *San Felipe*, a galleon of 2,000 tons burden, the naval wonder of the age, in respect of which, he says, he esteemed the other galleys but as wasps. Amongst the English the great struggle seems to have been who should be foremost in the fight. Once, the commander of another ship, whilst Ralegh was too busy to look behind him, secretly fastened a rope on to Ralegh's ship, so as to draw himself up equally with him; but Ralegh, being warned of this by one of his company, caused the rope to be cut. The victory was soon won. Two of the great galleons were captured; but Ralegh's desire "to shake hands" with the *San Felipe* was thwarted. It and another galleon were run aground, and blown up by their commanders, that they might not fall into English hands. But in this way many Spanish soldiers were destroyed. "The spectacle," writes Ralegh, "was very lamentable on their side; for many drowned themselves; many, half burnt, leapt into the water; very many hanging by the ropes' ends by the ship's side under the water, even to the lips; many swimming with grievous wounds, strucken under water, and put out of their pain; and withal so huge a fire and such tearing of the ordinance in the great *Felipe* and the rest when the fire came to them, as, if any man had a desire to see hell itself, it was there most lively figured."

The fleet was beaten in little over three hours; then the English landed their forces, and attacked the town. Ralegh was severely wounded in the leg; but he had himself carried ashore on men's shoulders to see how things were going. He was not able to remain more than an hour in the town, for the torment that he suffered from his wound. He returned to take charge of the fleet, as there was no admiral left on board, and he himself was unfit for anything but rest at that time. The town was carried " with a sudden fury, and with little loss." By the evening it was in the hands of the English, and early the next morning the citadel capitulated.

At break of day Ralegh sent to the Admiral for orders to follow the fleet of ships bound for the Indies, which lay in the roads of Puerto Real; but Howard and Essex were too busy to attend to him. It was a great mistake not to take vigorous steps to complete the victory by the capture of this great fleet. Ralegh saw what ought to be done, but could get none to second him. In the afternoon the merchants of Cadiz and Seville offered the Generals two millions to spare the fleet. "Whereupon," says Ralegh, "there was nothing done for the present." Meanwhile, much of the merchandize on board the ships was being carried on land by the Spanish sailors; and early next morning the Duke of Medina-Sidonia, the admiral of the fleet, whose pride could not brook the idea of his vessels falling into the hands of the English, ordered them to be set on fire, and all the mighty fleet of men-of-war and merchant-men were reduced to ashes. So the English lost the chance of gaining possession of this rich prize, though the loss to the Spaniards was as great as if the ships had been taken by the English.

Whilst the fleet was burning the English sol-diers were busy sacking the town. Orders were given that there should be no kind of violence or hard usage offered to any, either man, woman, or child, on pain of death. These orders seem to have been obeyed; except that the Dutch, who had done little in the fight, showed a desire to revenge themselves on the Spanish women and children for the horrible outrages committed by Spaniards in the Netherlands; but they were re-strained by the English. Howard wrote to the Queen's council: "The mercy and clemency that hath been showed here will be spoken of through-out the world; no aged or cold blood touched, no woman injured, but all with great care embarked and sent to St. Mary's Port; and other women and children were likewise sent thither, and suf-fered to carry away with them all their apparel, and divers rich things which they had about them, which no man might search for under pain of death." The town however was fired by Essex's orders in four quarters, and was left a smoking ruin.

Essex gave counsel that the English should hold the town of Cadiz, which would have been a perpetual thorn in Philip's side. The position of the city rendered this an easy task; but Howard would not consent. He had done as much as his orders allowed, and he would go no further. He knew that the Queen and Council at home would not second Essex in his desire for a prolonged war. Essex, much disgusted, had to give way. He next asked that the fleet might go round by the Azores, to intercept a rich fleet of Indiamen, which he knew was daily expected there. Howard would not consent to this either, but adhered strictly to his orders, and sailed back to England. The fleet reached Plymouth again on the 8th of August.

Ralegh had hurried back two days before the rest of the fleet, as there was much sickness on board his ship; so he brought the first news of the victory to the anxious Queen and Council. Writing to Sir Robert Cecil about the battle, he says, "The King of Spain was never so much dishonoured, neither hath he ever received so great loss. The Earl hath behaved himself, I protest unto you by the living God, both valiantly and advisedly in the highest degree; without pride, without cruelty, and hath gotten great honour and much love of all. I hope her most excellent Majesty will take my labours and endeavours in good part. Other riches than the hope thereof I have none; only I have received a blow, which now I thank God is well amended, only a little eyesore will remain. If my life had ended withal, I had then paid some part of the great debts which I owe her. But it is but borrowed; and I shall pay it, I hope, to her Majesty's advantage, if occasion be offered."

The spoils on this occasion were not nearly so great as the Court had hoped; and disappointment on this account diminished the cordiality with which the victors were received by the Queen. There was, as usual, much quarrelling over the spoils; and those who had done the most probably got the least. On this point Ralegh writes: "What the Generals have gotten I know least; they protest it is little. For my own part I have gotten a lame leg and a deformed. I have not wanted good words, and exceeding kind and regardful usance; but I have possession of naught but poverty and pain."

Though some might be disappointed at the smallness of the spoils, others could see the great importance of this victory. A third of the King of Spain's navy, and a great city with its citadel, had been destroyed in thirty-six hours by the audacity of a small fleet of English and Dutch. The loss to Philip II. was enormous; and once more a stop was put to the growth of his power. Essex and Ralegh, and others of the younger nobles, were eager to go on; hatred to Spain burnt as fiercely as ever in their breasts, and they longed to crush her utterly. But Elizabeth was old and worn out, and could no longer share their young enthusiasm; peace was what she wanted, and now that England was safe, she would consent to no more war.

Even now Ralegh was not allowed to resume his duties as Captain of the Guard; but he continued on good terms with Essex and Cecil. His relations with Cecil may be judged from the tone of a letter which he wrote to Cecil on the death of his wife. It is worth while to quote some portions of this on account of the light which it throws upon the character of the writer. It shows his strength and firmness, and how clearly he saw that a man must be self-summed, not swayed by every blast of passion; but that, taking life as a whole, he must look upon it as something out of which he has to make the best he can for himself and for others.

"It apertaineth," he writes, "to every man of a wise and worthy spirit to draw together into sufferance the unknown future to the known present, looking no less with the eyes of the mind than those of the body, the one beholding afar off, the other at hand; that those things of this world in which we live be not strange unto us when they approach, as to feebleness, which is moved with novelties. But that like true men participating immortality, and knowing our destinies to be of God, we do then make our estates and wishes, our fortunes and desires, all one. It is true that you have lost a good and virtuous wife, and myself an honourable friend and kinswoman. But there was a time when she was unknown to you, for whom you lamented then not. She is now no more yours nor of your acquaintance, but immortal, and not needing or knowing your love or sorrow. Therefore you shall but grieve for that which now is as then it was, when not yours; only bettered by the difference in this, that she hath passed the wearisome journey of this dark world, and hath possession of her inheritance.

"I believe that sorrows are dangerous companions, converting bad into evil and evil into worse, and do no other service than multiply harms. They are the treasures of weak hearts and of the foolish. The mind that entertaineth them is as the earth and dust, whereon sorrows and adversities of the world do—as the beasts of the field—tread, trample, and defile. The mind of man is that part of God which is in us, which by how much it is subject to passion, by so much it is farther from Him that gave it us. Sorrows draw not the dead to life, but the living to death. And if I were myself to advise myself in the like, I would never forget my patience till I saw all and the worst of evils, and so grieve for all at once, lest lamenting for some one, another might not remain in the power of destiny of greater discomfort.—Yours ever beyond the power of words to utter,   "W. RALEGH."

Ralegh seems to have continued his efforts to bring about peaceful intercourse between Essex

and Cecil. Essex had been much disgusted by
discovering on his return from Cadiz that in his
absence Cecil had been made Secretary. This advancement of Cecil shows how Elizabeth's head
was stronger than her heart. She knew that it
would be thoroughly displeasing to the favourite
whom she fondly loved; but she knew also that
Cecil would prove a useful servant, and in this
she was not disappointed. Sir Robert Cecil was
not a great man; but he was wise and cautious.
He had been educated as a statesman, and, as a
natural consequence, lacked originality. Diligent
and conscientious, he had not a spark of genius,
and could not appreciate it in others. He
seems to have wished to serve his Queen and
country honestly, whilst keeping his eye on his
own advantage. He was a stumbling-block in
the way of Essex, as his father had been in the
way of Leicester. He had no real sympathy
with Ralegh, and could not enter into his views;
but as long as it served his purpose, he kept on
friendly terms with him. He was too prudent
ever to show hostility to any man, and too courteous ever to treat anyone with insolence, and so,
without any conscious hypocrisy, he may have
seemed to Ralegh and his wife a truer friend than
he afterwards proved to be.

Cecil warmly followed his father in his desire
for peace, and his appointment as Secretary had
greatly increased the strength of the peace party.
In his opposition to the peace party Essex seems

for a time to have forgotten other animosities, and to have made no objections to Ralegh's return to favour at Court. In a letter to Sir Robert Sidney, then governor of Flushing, written by a certain Rowland Whyte, who kept Sidney supplied with news from London, dated April 9th, 1597, we read : " Sir W. Ralegh is daily in Court, and a hope is that he shall be admitted to the execution of his office as Captain of the Guard before his going to sea. His friends, you know, are of the greatest authority and power here, and Essex gives it no opposition, his mind being full, and only carried away with the business he hath in his head of conquering and overcoming the enemy." Another letter of Whyte's, written June 21st, says : " Yesterday my Lord of Essex rode to Chatham. In his absence Sir Walter Ralegh was brought to the Queen by Cecil, who used him very graciously, and gave him full authority to execute his place as Captain of the Guard, which immediately he undertook, and swore many men into the places void. In the evening he rode abroad with the Queen, and had private·conference with her; and now he comes boldly to the Privy Chamber as he was wont. Though this was done in the absence of the Earl, yet is it known that it was done with his liking and furtherance."

So, after five years of disgrace, Ralegh was once more favoured with the royal smile; and at this time his power and importance at Court seem to have been great. In 1597 Elizabeth yielded to

the entreaties of Essex, and gave permission for
another attack upon Spain. It was said that
Philip was fitting out a new Armada wherewith to invade England. Ralegh wrote a paper
on these reports, called *Opinion on the Spanish
Alarum*, in which he discussed the best means
for defending the coast, but expressed his doubts
as to the possibility of the King of Spain being
in readiness for so great an undertaking. He
was as eager as anyone for an attack upon Spain.
A fleet was fitted out, of which Essex was appointed admiral and general-in-chief, whilst Lord
Thomas Howard commanded one squadron, and
Ralegh another. A Dutch squadron also joined
the fleet.

A Spanish fleet was supposed to be preparing
in Ferrol, a port on the north coast of Spain, for
a descent upon Ireland, where the Spaniards hoped
to find plenty of support from the disaffected
Irish. The object of Essex and Ralegh was to
attack Ferrol, to destroy the ships there, and also
to intercept a rich fleet of Indiamen on its way
to Spain. The departure of the English fleet was
delayed for a long while by contrary winds. They
set sail on the 10th of July, 1597, and fell in
with a tremendous storm, which lasted five days.
"The storm so increased," writes Ralegh, "and
the billows so raised and enraged as we could
carry no sail. . . . On Saturday night we made
accompt to have yielded ourselves up to God."
The fleet had to put back to Plymouth much

disabled. One by one the ships came in, each in a more miserable condition than the last. Essex would not return till he was in imminent peril of sinking in the sea. Ralegh, on reaching Plymouth, wrote to Cecil his fears "that my Lord General himself will wrestle with the seas to his peril, or (constrained to come back) be found utterly heart-broken." Essex was in truth much cast down by these reverses. But the ships were repaired, though they had been so severely damaged that Ralegh wrote of them: "We shall not be in any great courage for winter weather and long nights in these ships."

Contrary winds prevailed for some time; but, on the 18th August, at last a fresh start was made. A few days after starting, the fleet was again scattered by another storm. Ralegh and his squadron were missing, and the wind blew straight out of Ferrol, which made any further undertaking against that place hopeless. The next thing to be done was to attempt the capture of the fleet of Indiamen, and for this purpose Essex sailed to the Azores, hoping to meet Ralegh there.

Ralegh meanwhile had been spending an anxious time; for his ship had been damaged in the storm. He wrote to Cecil: "I have never dared to rest since my wrecks, and, God doth judge, I never for these ten days came so much as into bed or cabin." Essex contrived to send to Ralegh by a pinnace a message to follow him to the islands, and there at last they met again off the Island of

Flores. Sir Christopher Blount, a bitter opponent of Ralegh's, and certain other officers, had been doing their utmost to excite Essex's anger against Ralegh, by making all kinds of insinuations as to his doings. Sir Arthur Gorges, who was with Ralegh, gives an account of their meeting, and says "that the Earl seemed the joyfullest man living for our arrival." He told Ralegh "the many conjectures and surmises that had been vented of his absence, and withal named to¹ him some of those men who had taxed him secretly with strange reports, yet pretended to love him." According to Gorges, Essex felt very high esteem for Ralegh. "In his (Essex's) greatest actions of service, and in the times of his chiefest recreations, he would ever accept of his counsel and company before many others who thought themselves more in favour."

From information brought to him by a pinnace just come from the Indies, Essex judged it unlikely that the fleet of Indiamen would pass that way. He therefore determined to take possession of some of the islands, and lay them waste, as they were the chief places where the Spanish ships coming from the Indies rested and refreshed themselves. Essex and Ralegh were to attack the Isle of Fayal, which had the best fort; whilst others of the islands were attacked by other commanders. Ralegh's men were still busy getting in water and refreshing themselves on land, when Essex sailed for Fayal, bidding Ralegh follow as soon as possible. Ralegh followed in all haste, and reached Fayal before Essex. He found it to be a fine town, pleasantly situated on the shore, with a strong citadel. The inhabitants, as soon as they saw the hostile ships, began to take measures for their safety, sending their women and children, and as much property as possible, up into the country.

Ralegh's men were impatient for the attack; but Ralegh knew that Essex would think his dignity deeply wounded if they began before he arrived. They waited two days, their impatience hourly increasing: they were in want of fresh water, and it seemed weary work to wait there, cooped up in their little ships, when before them lay a fair town and a most delightful country, abundantly provided with all they needed. Besides this, the delay was diminishing their chance of booty, by giving the inhabitants time to carry off their property. At last, after two days, Ralegh called a council of war, and then it was agreed, after much debating, to wait one day more, and then, if Essex did not come, to make the attack.

The next day was the fourth after their arrival at Fayal, and still Essex did not come; so Ralegh proceeded with two hundred and sixty men to effect a landing. Some of the Netherlanders who had arrived wished to assist him, but Ralegh would not hear of it. As his boats drew near the shore they were greeted with such a shower of shot from the citadel that the men grew dismayed. Even

Ralegh's reproachful outcries could not urge them
on till he ordered his boatmen to row his own
barge full upon the rocks, bidding those follow
him who dared. At last a landing was effected,
and then they were joined by some of the Dutch
soldiers, so that Ralegh had about six hundred
men under his command. He determined to advance straight upon the town and fort, instead of
trying to gain an easier entrance by a circuitous
march; for the day was hot, and his men were in
urgent need of supplies. As he advanced however, his men, to Ralegh's great distress, began to
break their ranks under the enemy's fire. He determined to try and make others brave by doing
that which they dared not do. Accompanied only
by eight or ten men, he went forward to discover
the best way to mount the hill. All the while
the shot of the enemy flew thick about him. Sir
Arthur Gorges, who was with him, had his left leg
shot through with a musket ball, and Ralegh himself was shot through his breeches and doublet
sleeves in two or three places.

When he had found out all that he wanted he
gave orders for his men to follow him. He expected an engagement outside the town, but the
enemy retired at his approach; and on entering the
town he saw that the inhabitants had fled, taking
with them all they could. The English found it a
very pleasant town, with beautiful gardens full of
fruit and plenty of fresh water. Here they reposed
all night. The next morning before break of day

the Earl of Essex was seen bearing down with full sail upon the town.

As soon as possible those amongst Ralegh's companions who were jealous of his fame hastened on board the general's ship, and did their utmost to fill him with anger at Ralegh's presumption in attacking the town before his arrival. It was not difficult to rouse Essex's jealousy; and when Ralegh, who had put off from the town in his barge, landed on board the general's ship, he was received on all sides with estranged looks, and the Earl, after giving him a faint welcome, began at once to upbraid him with his breach of orders. Ralegh defended his conduct, and managed to pacify Essex a little. His enemies however did their utmost to fan the quarrel, saying that Ralegh ought to be tried by court-martial, and lose his head for disobedience to the general's orders. The wise words of Lord Thomas Howard finally brought about a reconciliation, though Essex never seems to have got over his irritation against Ralegh for carrying off all the glory of this "Island voyage," as it was called.

Before leaving Fayal they fired the town; and after waiting about a little longer, in hope of falling in with the Indian fleet, they proceeded homewards. On the way back several prizes were captured; but the luck was not with Essex. The chief prizes fell into Ralegh's hands, and Essex came home in a jealous and disappointed frame of mind. The expedition had been a failure; the

Spanish fleet at Ferrol had not been destroyed, and the Indiamen had not been captured. The only success had been won by Ralegh, who was now taken back into full favour by the Queen. Essex, on the contrary, was greeted with reproaches for the failure of the expedition.

The elevation of the Lord High Admiral, Charles Lord Howard of Effingham, to the dignity of Earl of Nottingham, was a new and bitter grievance to Essex. As he was now also an earl, Howard was able, as Lord High Admiral, to take precedence over Essex; and Essex could so little endure this, that he kept away from Court and Council altogether. He did not try to disguise his anger, and so roused the Queen's indignation. But she could not get on without him for long, and many attempts were made to pacify him. At last Essex was made Earl-Marshal of England, which gave him back his old precedence over Nottingham, who retired from Court in disgust.

Before Essex returned to England, the Spanish fleet actually sailed from Ferrol with the object of making a descent upon the English coast. But the same storm which met Essex and Ralegh on their way back from the Azores scattered and in great part destroyed the Spanish fleet, which was obliged to put back to Ferrol.

CHAPTER IX.

Last Days of Elizabeth.

THE year after the "Island voyage," in 1598,
Elizabeth's chief enemy, Philip II., died, at
the age of seventy-one. His great schemes had
not succeeded. He had lost the Netherlands, and
had failed to establish the power of his house.
He had expended such enormous sums of money
in the furtherance of his schemes that, in spite of
the wealth he received from his colonies, he left
his country financially ruined. After his death
the power of Spain in Europe steadily though
slowly declined. But it was formidable enough,
and the voices of Essex and Ralegh were still for
war. Burleigh and others hoped to establish a
lasting peace, which might diminish the Queen's
difficulties in Ireland, where the rebels always
looked to Spain for help. Early in 1598, Henry
IV. of France had made peace with Philip II.;
and France, under a king of Huguenot blood, if
no longer of Huguenot faith, was at last enjoying
the blessings of peace and toleration. Elizabeth
had long carried on the struggle against Spain;

and she too in her old age wished for peace. But Irish difficulties were again pressing on her, and there were many debates in council how they should be met. Ralegh had thought much on Irish affairs, and knew more about the difficulties of government in Ireland than most men about the Queen. She often asked his advice; but she would not make him what he so much wished to be—a member of her council. Ralegh longed to shine as a statesman, and would undoubtedly have done so had he been permitted; but the jealousy of his enemies kept him from holding any important office in the State.

In the debates in council on Irish affairs Essex expressed his opinions with violence, especially in the discussion about filling up the vacant office of lord-deputy. On one occasion, when the Queen would not listen to him, he so far forgot the respect he owed her as to turn his back upon her in contempt. This was too much for Elizabeth, who, in a fit of rage, gave him a box on the ear, and bade him "Go, and be hang'd." Essex laid his hand upon his sword, exclaiming that he would not have put up with such an affront, not at the hands of Henry VIII. himself, and left the Court in a passion.

Before long a reconciliation was brought about; but it is said that Elizabeth never quite forgot the affront. On August 4th, 1598, she lost her faithful and well-tried servant, William Cecil, Lord Burleigh, who died at the age of seventy-eight, having

served Elizabeth for forty years. During the whole
of this time he had been her chief adviser and
guide, the very soul of her policy. His death left
her lonely, surrounded by younger men whose
enthusiasm she could not share, who had not
gone through the days of struggle, difficulty, and
danger with her. England was going on and
leaving her behind; it was no longer the England
she had known, and loved, and guided through
storm and peril. The results of her work were
beginning to be seen; but she could not understand them. Men were thinking of her successor;
and though she herself would not allow the subject to be discussed, she knew that it was in
everyone's thoughts. Essex, the man she most
loved, treated her rudely and contemptuously, and
yet she still clung to him. She tried to disguise
her age by paint and false hair. She is described
by a foreign ambassador about this time as having
"an oblong face, fair but wrinkled; her eyes small,
yet black and pleasant; her nose a little hooked;
her lips narrow, and her teeth black. She had in
her ears two pearls, with very rich drops; she
wore false hair, and that red; upon her head a
small crown. Her bosom was uncovered, as all
the English ladies have it till they marry. She
had on a necklace of exceeding fine jewels; her
hands were small, her fingers long, and her stature
neither tall nor low; her air was stately; her
manner of speaking mild and obliging. She was
dressed in white silk, bordered with pearls of the

size of beans, and over it a mantle of black silk shot with silver threads. Her train was very long, the end of it borne by a marchioness; instead of a chain she had an oblong collar of gold and jewels." But false hair and fine dresses could not make Elizabeth a young beauty; and we cannot wonder that Essex was always fretting against the chains in which she tried to hold him, and struggled after a more active life, which would better suit his ambitious spirit.

At last it was determined to send Essex himself as lord-deputy to Ireland, with an army of 22,000 men, to quell the rebellion of the Earl of Tyrone. It was thought that there Essex would find a field for his warlike energies. He himself went rather unwillingly; he was afraid of what his enemies might do in his absence; but the people, with whom he was always a favourite on account of his princely generosity, greeted his appointment with enthusiasm, and hoped great things from it.

Since the defeat and death of the Earl of Desmond, Ireland had been nominally at peace; but the severity of the government, and the cruelty and exactions of the soldiers, had fostered the spirit of discontent amongst the Irish. Spanish agents and Jesuits in disguise had done their utmost to increase this discontent. Ireland was then, as it has ever been, England's most vulnerable point; and it was very important to Spain to keep Ireland in an unsettled condition. At last, in 1592, the discontent broke out in the rebellion of Hugh O'Neill, the Earl of Tyrone, round whom gathered the northern tribes.

Elizabeth had done her utmost to secure the fidelity of Hugh O'Neill. He had been partly educated at the English Court, and she had given him the earldom of Tyrone. For a time he had been a faithful supporter of the government; but when his power increased, he determined to assert his independence. His rebellion had now reached such formidable proportions that it was absolutely necessary to suppress it; and this was the work with which Essex was entrusted.

By his conduct in Ireland Essex disappointed everyone's hopes. His orders had been to proceed at once against Tyrone; but he spent three months in desultory warfare before he marched against him at all. Then his soldiers were so dispirited by sickness that he did not venture to risk a battle. He concluded an armistice with Tyrone against express orders, and hastened back to England, trusting to his popularity and favour with the Queen to prevent his conduct from being too severely censured. There were rumours of a renewal of the war with Spain, and this made him doubly anxious to be in England again. On his arrival at Court he burst in upon the Queen when she least expected him. In her surprise she received him at first with affection; but presently ordered him to his apartment, and expressed her displeasure at his disobedience of her orders. Essex's enemies now had a real charge against him.

They even accused him of having made a treaty with Tyrone, with a view of obtaining his aid in a projected rising. His conduct was examined by the Council, and he was committed to custody. The Queen was extremely irritated against him. She said, "I am no Queen. That man is above me. Who gave him command to come here so soon? I did send him on other business." Finally Essex was deprived of his offices, and bidden to live a prisoner in his own house during the Queen's pleasure. He allowed his anger against the Queen to vent itself in violent language, which, when repeated to her, only increased her irritation. His enemies were always at hand to prevent any relenting on her part. Ralegh and Cecil were probably both equally anxious to bring about Essex's ruin. They seem to have been on very good terms with one another at this time. We find that Cecil's young son was being educated at Sherborne, with Ralegh's son Walter, under the care of Lady Ralegh.

At one time Ralegh seems to have feared lest Cecil might be persuaded to relent towards Essex, and he wrote a letter warning Cecil in strong language against such a course. "I am not wise enough to give you advice," he writes; "but if you take it for good counsel to relent towards this tyrant, you will repent it when it shall be too late. His malice is fixt, and will not evaporate by any your mild courses. For he will ascribe the alteration to her Majesty's pusilanimity,

and not to your good nature; knowing that you
work but upon her humour, and not out of any
love towards him. The less you make him, the
less he shall be able to harm you and yours.
And if her Majesty's favour fail him, he will again
decline to a common person. . . . Lose not your
advantage," he concludes; "if you do, I read your
destiny." This letter is that of a clear-sighted,
ambitious man, who allows no scruples to stand
between himself and the attainment of his purposes. Ralegh, Cecil, and Cecil's brother-in-law,
Lord Henry Cobham, were looked upon as the
chief enemies of Essex at Court, and for the time
their influence was supreme.

In 1600 a monopoly for the sale of sweet wines
possessed by Essex fell in, and the Queen did not
renew it. Essex seems then to have lost all hope
of returning to favour. He determined to risk
everything, and, trusting to his popularity, to attempt by force to regain his old influence in state
affairs. He seems to have cherished a wild plan
of seizing the Queen's person, and ruling in her
name. He summoned his friends to Essex House,
and there held frequent conferences with them,
till at last the government grew alarmed, and summoned Essex to appear before the Privy Council.
He excused himself on the ground of indispo-
sition, and, seeing the suspicion with which he
was looked upon, determined to make his attempt
at once. The force of the conspirators was too
small to enable them to attack the Court; but the

plan was that Essex, at the head of two hundred
gentlemen, should ride through the streets of the
City, and stir up the people to rise in his favour,
and deliver him from his enemies, especially from
Ralegh and Cobham, who, he asserted, constantly
threatened his life.

The night before this desperate attempt, Ralegh,
who was then in his town-house, Durham House,
in the Strand, sent for Sir Ferdinando Gorges to
come and speak with him. Gorges had served
often under both Essex and Ralegh, and was now
one of the conspirators in Essex House. Essex
bade him go and see Ralegh, only he advised him
not to go to Durham House, but to meet Ralegh
on the Thames. Sir Christopher Blount, another
of the conspirators, advised Gorges to take the
opportunity of killing Ralegh, advice which Gorges
scornfully rejected. Durham House had gardens
and stairs running down to the Thames, and
Ralegh came out in a boat alone to meet Gorges,
who came from Essex House, which was also on
the Thames, bringing two gentlemen with him.
Ralegh's object seems to have been to try and
detach Gorges from the conspiracy, and he advised
him "to depart the town presently." But Gorges
replied that it was too late; that there were "two
thousand gentlemen who had resolved that day to
live or die freemen." He bade Sir Walter go back
to the Court; "for he was like to have a bloody
day of it." They parted after a fruitless interview, and Ralegh rowed back in haste; for a boat

came from the stairs of Essex House, containing some of the Earl's servants, who had orders either to seize or kill Ralegh.

The next morning, 8th February, 1601, Essex made his foolish attempt. Some of the members of Council came early to Essex House in the hope of stopping the rising peaceably; but they were kept as hostages. Essex opened his gates, and riding out at the head of two hundred gentlemen, made his way into the City. There, with shouts of "For the Queen! My life is in danger!" he tried to rouse the citizens to arms. He told them that his life was threatened by the daggers of Ralegh, Cecil, and Cobham, and that he wished to free the Queen from the evil councillors by whom she was surrounded. But the people simply gazed in amazement, and no one stirred. At last Essex plainly saw that his cause was desperate. He made his way back to his house, and that night was obliged to surrender to the Earl of Nottingham. The next morning he was taken to the Tower.

In a few days Essex was brought to trial for high treason before a body of twenty-five peers. One of his chief associates, the Earl of Southampton, Shakspeare's patron and friend, was tried with him. Both pleaded not guilty. Essex tried to defend himself by accusing others. He asserted that Ralegh and Cobham had meant to murder him in his own house. He said of Cecil that he favoured the claim of the Spanish Infanta to the

English crown. With greater justice he accused Francis Bacon, who appeared against him as Queen's Counsel, of perfidy and base ingratitude.

Francis Bacon was the son of Sir Nicholas Bacon, who had been Elizabeth's Lord-Keeper till 1579, and had been amongst the greatest of the statesmen who gathered round her throne. His death had called back his son Francis from Paris, where he was completing his education in the house of the English Ambassador, Sir Amias Paulet. Francis had wished to devote himself to literature and politics; but he had no private means, and the death of his father left him without a friend in the government from whom he could hope for advancement. It is true that Lord Burleigh was his uncle; for Burleigh and Sir Nicholas Bacon had each married one of the learned daughters of Sir Anthony Coke. But Burleigh was anxious for the advancement of his own son Robert, who was just the same age as Francis, and looked with jealousy on his nephew, in whom he could not fail to see far greater genius than in his own son. At last Francis found a friend and patron in the Earl of Essex. Essex never did anything by halves; and he proved a very warm friend. Bacon had devoted himself to the study of the law. When the office of Attorney-General fell vacant, Essex did his utmost to procure it for Bacon; when that was filled up, he tried to get him the office of Solicitor-General. When he failed in this too,

he tried to make up for it by personal kindness.
But no remembrance of the past prevented Bacon
from agreeing to appear as counsel for the prosecution at Essex's trial.   He had no wish to injure
Essex, but he had a strong fear of injuring his
own prospects.   He did not want to ally his
fortunes with those of the fallen favourite; and
not content with abstaining from appearing as his
friend, he did his utmost to blacken his character.
In his speech at Essex's trial he employed all his
wit and talent to set the Earl's conduct in the
worst light possible.

Essex was condemned on the same principle
which had led to the conviction of the Duke
of Norfolk and Mary Queen of Scots—the principle that every attempt at rebellion must be
looked upon as directed against the life of the
ruling sovereign.   Elizabeth went through a hard
struggle before she could make up her mind to
sign his death-warrant.   But she who had allowed
the execution of Mary Queen of Scots could not
now go against the laws of England to save the
life of the man she loved best.

Before he was brought to execution Essex was
led, by the influence of religion, to confess his
guilt; and he made known a correspondence in
which he had been engaged with the King of
Scots.   From this it appeared that he had managed
to gain James to his side by affirming that Cecil
and others were prepared to maintain the Spanish
claim to the succession.   This probably greatly

aggravated Elizabeth's anger against him; for though she must have known that James VI. of Scotland would be her successor, she would never acknowledge him as such, and in general hated any allusion to the succession.

Essex was executed on the 25th February, 1601. The life of the Earl of Southampton was spared; but he was kept a prisoner in the Tower for the rest of Elizabeth's reign. Sir Christopher Blount and three other followers of Essex were also executed. At Blount's execution Ralegh was present in his capacity as Captain of the Guard. Blount had been one of Ralegh's bitterest enemies; and now, before he laid his head on the block, he asked, "Is Sir Walter Ralegh here?" and when Ralegh came forward, he said, "Sir Walter Ralegh, I thank God that you are present. I had an infinite desire to speak with you to ask your forgiveness ere I died. Both for the wrong done to you, and for my particular ill-intent towards you, I beseech you forgive me." Ralegh answered, "I most willingly forgive you; and I beseech God to forgive you, and to give you His divine comfort."

Ralegh's chief adversaries at Court were gone; but he did not on that account gain a more important position in State affairs. In September, 1600, he had been made Governor of Jersey, and he set out at once to visit the island. Lady Ralegh wrote to Cecil about his journey: "He was two days and two nights on the sea with contrary winds; notwithstanding he went from Weymouth with so fair wind and weather, as little Wat and myself brought him aboard the ship. He writeth to me he never saw a pleasanter island, but protesteth unfeignedly it is not in value the very third part that was reported." Ralegh did not look upon his governorship as a sinecure, and did all he could to increase the prosperity of Jersey. He busied himself with securing the fortifications of the island; he founded a trade between Jersey and Newfoundland, and did his utmost to remove the abuses and oppressions of the government of Jersey.

In 1601 Ralegh went with the Queen on progress. He seems to have left her and come back to London to receive the French Ambassador, the Duke of Biron, who had been sent over to consult with the Queen about new aggressions on the part of the Spaniards. From London Ralegh writes to Cecil: "I am glad I came hither; for I never saw so great a person so neglected." He proceeded to do his utmost for the entertainment of the French envoy. "We have carried them to Westminster to see the monuments, and this Monday we entertained them at the bear-garden which they had great pleasure to see." As soon as horses could be provided the Duke of Biron was taken to the Vine, a country house near Basing, in Hampshire, where the Queen was staying. Here the Queen caused him to be magnificently entertained; plate and hangings were brought from

Hampton Court to make the house fit for his reception. Elizabeth had hoped that a personal interview between herself and Henry IV. of France, at Dover, might have been arranged. Henry sent instead his most trusted Minister, the Duke of Sully, to discuss with Elizabeth the means to be taken against Spain and the house of Austria generally.

In 1601, Elizabeth opened her last Parliament. The people had not forgiven her the death of her favourite Essex, and as she passed through the streets on her way to the House she was not greeted with the same enthusiastic shouts as of old. The world seemed very gloomy to her; for she had never got over the shock of her favourite's conspiracy and death. The tone of the Parliament which now met must have helped to show her that a new state of things was beginning which she was not able to meet. She could not understand the result of her own work. She had by her caution gained for her people the means of living in freedom, and now they wished to use the freedom which her rule had developed. But her proud Tudor spirit found it next to impossible to bow before the will of Parliament. Till now, by strict economy, she had managed to be almost independent of parliamentary grants, and so had asserted her superiority over Parliament. Now large supplies were needed for the Irish wars, and the knowledge that the Crown required these supplies gave Parliament more courage in speaking out than it had shown before in this reign.

Ralegh had been in Parliament since 1585. He had soon begun to take an active part in the business of the House, and had made himself very useful on committees. When the question of the subsidies came on, he spoke strongly on the necessity of granting liberally, seeing that Spanish forces were actually in Ireland, and that "the sale of her Majesty's own jewels; the great loans her subjects have lent her yet unpaid; the continual selling of her lands and decaying of her revenues; the sparing even out of her own purse and her own apparel for our own sakes, will not serve." All were agreed that the subsidy must be granted; but there was some little difference as to how it was to be levied. Cecil talked loudly of the willingness which everyone should show to contribute. "Neither pots nor pans, nor dish nor spoon, should be spared when danger is at our elbows. . . . He would have the King of Spain know how willing we are to sell all in defence of God's religion, our prince, and our country." Bacon concluded a speech with, "*Dulcis tractus pari jugo* (it is easy to draw with equal yoke); therefore the poor as well as the rich ought not to be exempted." Ralegh showed his farsightedness and his sense of justice by his answer. "I like it not that the Spaniards, our enemies, should know of our selling our pots and pans to pay subsidies. Well may you call it policy, as an honourable person alledged; but I am sure it argues poverty in the state. And for the motion that was last made, *dulcis tractus pari jugo;* call you this *par jugum* (equal yoke) when a poor man pays as much as a rich? and peradventure his estate is no better than it is set at, or but little better; while our estates are three or four pounds in the Queen's books, and it is not the hundredth part of our wealth; therefore it is neither *dulcis* nor *par*." Unfortunately the sum of money wanted was so large that it had to be levied from both rich and poor.

When the question of the subsidy was settled, the House proceeded, on the 20th November, to make a complaint against monopolies. These monopolies were the means by which the Queen rewarded her favourites, and were heavy burdens upon the people. The growing boldness of Parliament is shown by its daring to raise its voice against them. One member spoke of a "country that groaned under the burden of monstrous and unconscionable substitutes to monopolitans of starch, tin, fish, cloth, oil, vinegar, salt, and what not." Ralegh rose to answer as regarded tin; and stated that since he had held the office of Lord-Warden of the Stannaries the wages of the workmen in the tin mines had increased from two shillings a week to four shillings. "There is no poor that will work there but may, and have that wages;" but he ended by saying, "Yet if all others may be repealed, I will give

my consent as freely to the cancelling of this as
any member of this House." The advisers of the
Crown met the complaints by saying that the
granting of monopolies was a branch of the prerogative. But the House was determined. A
petition on the subject was sent to the Queen,
who saw the wisdom of giving way. She promised
to revoke all illegal patents, and her concession
was received by the House with extravagant rejoicings. Her promise, however, does not seem to
have been strictly carried out.

On several occasions during this session Ralegh
spoke out strongly for the freedom of the individual. An act was brought in to compel men
to sow a certain proportion of hemp on their
land; and Ralegh, speaking on this point, said,
"For my part I do not like this constraining of
men to manure or use their ground at our wills,
but rather let every man use his ground to that
which it is most fit for, and therein use his
own discretion." The bill was thrown out, and
later on it was proposed to repeal the Bill of
Tillage, made in a time of dearth, according to
which every man was obliged to plough the third
part of his land. Ralegh spoke in favour of the
repeal: "Many poor men," he said, "are not able
to find seed to sow so much ground as they are
bound to plough, which they must do or incur the
penalty of the law. Besides, all nations abound
with corn. . . . And therefore I think the best
course is to set it at liberty, and leave every man

free, which is the desire of a true Englishman." These statements sound to us like truisms; but they were by no means looked upon as such in those days of monopolies, protection, and over-busy legislation on all points. Ralegh himself by no means fully adopted the principles of free trade. In this same Parliament he spoke in favour of restraining the export of ordnance, saying, "I am sure heretofore one ship of her Majesty's was able to beat ten Spaniards; but now, by reason of our own ordnance, we are hardly matched one by one. I say there is nothing does so much threaten the conquest of this kingdom as the transportation of ordnance." The same man who spoke so strongly for repeal of the Statute of Tillage was in favour of a bill forbidding the export of ordnance.

Ralegh also spoke with much force on a bill for the more diligent resort to church on Sundays. He opposed the bill, and showed how it must remain a dead letter, unless an enormous amount of work were thrown on the churchwardens, who would have to appear at the assizes to give information to the grand jury. He calculated that about four hundred and eighty persons would have to appear at each assize on this subject. "What great multitudes this will bring together," he exclaimed, " what quarrelling and danger may happen, besides giving authority to a mean churchwarden; how prejudicial this may be." The bill was finally thrown out by one vote.

Whilst Parliament was debating the question of

the subsidy, a new deputy, Lord Mountjoy, was
subduing the rebels in Ireland. He defeated the
joint forces of the Spaniards and Irish, and compelled Tyrone to submit. Tyrone's final submission
came in immediately after Elizabeth's death. She
had been failing in mind and body ever since the
execution of Essex. To the last she persisted in
taking her usual exercises of hunting and riding;
and when in March, 1603, she grew really ill, she
refused to take any sustenance or go to bed. Her
kinsman, Robert Carey, went to visit her about
this time, and says that he "found her sitting low
upon her cushions. She took me by the hand and
wrung it hard, and said, 'No, Robin, I am not
well' . . . and in her discourse she fetched not
so few as forty or fifty great sighs. I was grieved
to see her in this plight; for in all my lifetime I
never knew her fetch a sigh, but when the Queen
of Scots was beheaded." On the 23rd of March
she grew speechless, and on Thursday morning her
spirit passed away, after she had been supposed
to indicate by signs that she wished James VI. of
Scotland to succeed her.

So died the great Queen. She had done her work
well and nobly, though she could not understand
or enter into its results. Whatever may be said
of her personal failings, it is at least clear that
she had guided England wisely through troublous
times. How she had strengthened the people's
character was to be seen in ways she little dreamt
of—in the struggle for freedom against Charles I.

CHAPTER X.

Accession of James I.

A FEW hours after Elizabeth's death, a meeting
was held at Whitehall, consisting of the
Privy Councillors, such Peers as were in London,
the Lord Mayor, and a few other persons. To
them Cecil submitted a proclamation, which he
had prepared, announcing the accession of James
VI. of Scotland to the throne of England.

As Elizabeth had never married, the direct line
of Henry VIII. came to an end at her death. All
through her reign much anxiety had been caused
by uncertainty about the succession. Elizabeth
could never be persuaded to name her successor.
At first this policy was wise, especially during
the lifetime of Mary Queen of Scots. The recognition of a Catholic successor would have given a
dangerous head to the intrigues of Spain; the
recognition of any successor at all would have
created a centre for malcontents, and would have
weakened the Queen's position. But towards the
end of Elizabeth's reign much anxiety might have
been spared had the Queen clearly recognised

James VI. of Scotland as her successor. Still
the thought of any successor was distasteful to
her. She was afraid lest, if she acknowledged
the claim of James VI., he would try to interfere
with English affairs; and so she adhered to the
policy which had become a habit to her. But
her refusal to consider the question of the succession could not keep her subjects from doing so.
It was discussed in secret, books were written
about it, and many intrigues were carried on.

Many different claims were put forward. Essex
had accused Cecil of favouring the claim of the
Infanta Isabella, daughter of Philip II. But this
claim, though it was a good deal talked about,
obtained no countenance except from some of the
most violent Catholics. It had been put forward
by them, because they saw no other chance of
getting a Catholic sovereign. To find any grounds
for her claim, they had to trace her descent from
Eleanor, daughter of Henry II., who had married
Alphonso IX. of Castile. Few even of the Catholics would have been willing to recognise a
claim such as this, which ignored the rights of
the House of Tudor, and would have handed over
England to a foreigner. The real question lay
between the Houses of Suffolk and of Stuart,
which both sprung from sisters of Henry VIII.,
as will be seen in the genealogical table. The
parliamentary title belonged to the House of
Suffolk. An Act of Parliament had given Henry
VIII. the right of disposing of the succession

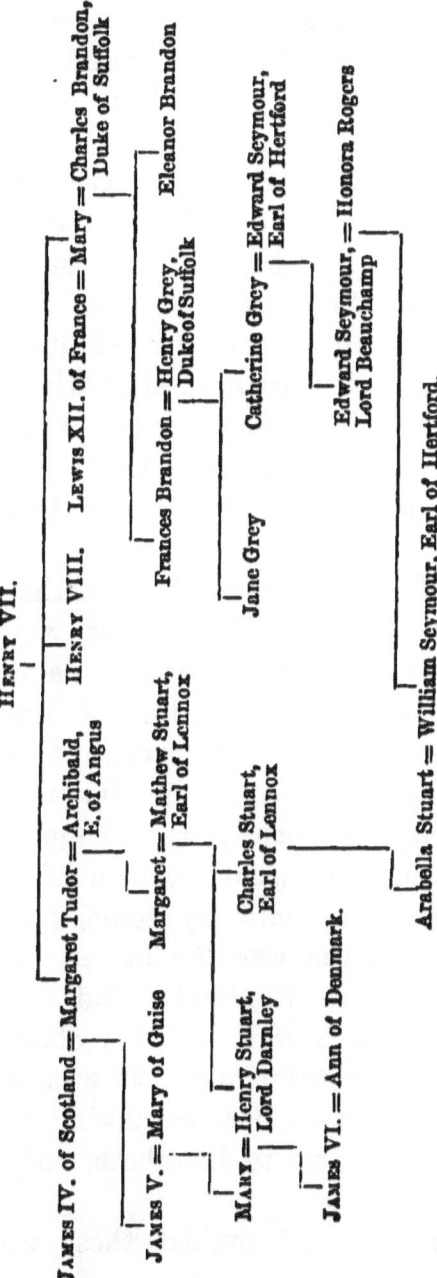

by will, and he had declared in his will that
after his own children and their issue the crown
should pass to the 'House of Suffolk. This will
led to the ill-fated attempt to place Lady Jane
Grey upon the throne. After her execution the
claim of the House of Suffolk passed to her
sister Catherine, and then to her son Lord
Beauchamp. But his claim had been rendered
doubtful by uncertainty as to the validity of his
parents' marriage. In reality, after the death
of Mary Queen of Scots had removed all fear
of the succession of a Roman Catholic, little
doubt remained as to the right of the House of
Stuart.

The House of Stuart derived its claim from
Margaret Tudor, Henry VIII.'s sister, who had
married James IV., king of Scotland. James VI.
of Scotland was the great grandson of Margaret
Tudor. But from time to time the claim had been
advanced of another descendant of Margaret's, by
her second marriage with the Earl of Angus. This
was Arabella Stuart, the second cousin of James
VI. An opinion was held by some, on legal
grounds, that her claim was the better, because
she had been born in England. But she was
without ambition for herself, and her claim was
never seriously brought forward. It was indeed
nothing but a burden to her by making her an
object of suspicion—first to Elizabeth, and then
to James.

It is not strange that amidst these various

claims men had looked forward to the death of Elizabeth as likely to produce serious disturbances. James himself had never dared to hope that he would succeed peaceably. He had tried to prepare the way for his succession by making a party for himself in England; and with this view had entered into correspondence with Essex and others, and had shown himself ready to take any steps which might ensure his succession. His correspondents, of course, took this opportunity of laying stress upon their own importance, and the use they might be to him, and of blackening the characters of their rivals at Court or in the government. One of the chief of these correspondents was Lord Henry Howard, Ralegh's bitterest enemy, and a man who thought no lie too base to be uttered, if he could only do harm to an enemy or advance himself. In his letters he indulged in the most venomous slanders against Ralegh, and managed to fill James's mind with suspicion and fear of him.

Amongst others, Robert Cecil entered into correspondence with James. He thought it wise to prevent him from taking any foolish steps with a view to ensuring his succession. He told him that if he would remain quiet, and do nothing rash, his succession would follow as a matter of course. James had been prejudiced against Cecil by Essex, who had always maintained that Cecil favoured the title of the Infanta. He was now delighted to find him amongst his friends. He

listened to his advice, and quietly bided his
time. Their correspondence was kept secret from
Elizabeth; but the knowledge of Cecil's support
sufficed to keep James from taking any unwise
steps.

News was at once sent to Edinburgh of Elizabeth's death, and of the proclamation of James.
All suspense was soon at an end; for by the 5th
of April letters were received from James con-
firming all officers in their places till he could
reach London.

James set out from Edinburgh on the 5th April.
On his way south every country house was thrown
open to him, and all kinds of festivities were prepared for his amusement. The English gentry,
accustomed to the elaborate manners which Elizabeth liked her courtiers to display, must have been
a little shocked at the appearance and manners of
James. His ungainly figure, his rolling walk, his
spluttering way of talking, were the reverse of
kingly; whilst his broad Scottish pronunciation
offended English ears. But he was good-humoured,
and full of desire to rule his kingdom well. Delighted with the warm reception with which he
met, he did his utmost to make himself agreeable
to his new subjects.

James was now in his thirty-seventh year, and
up till this time had been kept entirely under
the power of the Presbyterians in Scotland. Still
smarting under the restraints which he had endured at their hands, he came away from Scotland

with a strong dislike to Presbyterianism, and a
decided leaning to Episcopalianism. He had very
considerable intellectual powers, and his ambition
was to be regarded as the most learned man in
the two kingdoms. His knowledge and reading,
especially in theology, were considerable. He was
pedantic; but in those days, when the revival of
learning had opened up again the study of the
Greek and Latin languages, knowledge was apt to
make even the greatest students pedantic. The
new learning had not yet been brought into accord
with actual life. The possession of it seemed to
make a man something apart from his fellows.
James was shrewd, and possessed of strong com-
mon-sense. He could read other men's characters;
he could trace the causes of disorder and disturbance, and could lay down principles of calm wisdom, which he did not always apply to his own
conduct. He was constitutionally timorous, and
had no sympathy for the spirit of enterprise, the
love of energy and activity, which Elizabeth had
encouraged in her subjects. He wished to bind
men to him by personal favours, and get them
to do his will; not to take men as he found
them, and give them opportunities for using their
abilities for the good of their country. He was
himself incapable of a strong enthusiasm, or of a
noble passion, and could not understand it in
others. He had not the practical wisdom that
enabled Elizabeth to choose out men of merit for
state employment; to get every man about her

L

to do his best to distinguish himself in the eyes
of his sovereign and his country. He had a high
estimation of the royal power: it was in his reign
that the idea of the divine right of kings grew
up. He wished above all things to advance the
monarchy in England. He disliked Parliament;
for, as he once said, five hundred kings were as-
sembled there, and he thought it his duty to resist
its power. His influence on the fate of England
was very great; for his views gave the tone to the
policy of the House of Stuart—a policy which the
Englishmen whom Elizabeth, unconsciously to herself, had helped to nurture in the love of freedom
could not endure.

James's private life was strictly moral, but he
had not the strength of character to make his
Court moral. His one passion was for hunting,
though he was a bad rider, and this led him to
spend the greater part of the year in his country
seats. His leisure time was spent either in hunting
or in study; and in the midst of these occupations
at one of his country seats, great questions of
politics used to be discussed and settled. During
the first part of his reign the government was left
entirely in the hands of Cecil, who gained the
King's complete confidence. Cecil met James at
York on his way to London, and as no one knew
of the intercourse which had existed between the
two, everyone was surprised to see the cordiality
with which James greeted him. Men on all sides
flocked to meet the new King, till the Council

thought it wise to forbid the general resort to him.

Sir Walter Ralegh, as Captain of the Guard, went as far as Burghley, in Lincolnshire, to meet James. He had always believed that the accession of James was the best thing which could happen for England; but he had not entered into any correspondence with James. He had tried to speak to Cecil about James's accession; but Cecil had refused him his confidence, telling him that he for one had no intention of looking forward to such an event as his mistress's death.

Ralegh had no man at all his equal in position who shared his views, who could appreciate his genius, who would be willing to aid him in carrying out his great schemes. With the people he was extremely unpopular on account of his haughty manners; the great nobles regarded him as an adventurer; his equals in birth amongst the courtiers feared him as a dangerous rival. He does not seem to have been a lovable man; he was reserved and proud, and did not open himself out to many. It was only some of those who had served under him, and had gone through perils and difficulties with him, who seem to have learned what he really was, and clung to him with true devotion.

James was strongly prejudiced against him. Essex in his letters had done his utmost to prejudice the King's mind against his own opponents at Court; and when Cecil undeceived James's mind about himself, he made no attempt to do so about Ralegh.

It is difficult to understand what was exactly Cecil's attitude towards Ralegh. As long as Elizabeth lived he seems to have wished to behave to him as a firm and confidential friend. It is probable that in those days he looked upon him as a useful foil to Essex, and that he did not wish needlessly to quarrel with anyone who stood high in the Queen's estimation. But there was no real cordiality towards Ralegh in his heart. Cecil, a cautious, industrious man of business, could not understand Ralegh's fiery nature. He could feel no sympathy with his far-reaching views, and entirely failed to appreciate his genius. Ralegh's strength of character, his wide schemes, his grand ideas, seemed to him exaggerated. He thought him a dangerous character, as the small man often thinks a greater than himself to be. It was not difficult to make James look upon any one with suspicion. Essex, whom he greatly admired, had told him that Ralegh was a dangerous character, who in heart was opposed to his succession. It is a melancholy thought that these futile suspicions should have put a stop to Ralegh's active usefulness. Hardly past the prime of life, with full and mature experience, great knowledge, true patriotism, and a fertile mind ever devising new schemes for her advancement, it would be impossible to find a man who might be more useful to his King and country. But none of this brilliant promise was

to bear fruit; and in reality Ralegh's active life
ended with Elizabeth's death.

At Burghley, James I. received him coldly, and
greeted him with a stupid pun upon his name.
"By my saul, maun," he said, "I have heard but
rawly of thee." Ralegh did not stay long; he
needed royal letters to enable him to proceed in
some affairs connected with the duchy of Cornwall.
James bade his secretary hasten the preparation
of these letters, saying, "Let them be delivered
speedily, that Ralegh may be gone again." The
secretary wrote to Cecil, saying, "To my seeming,
Ralegh hath taken no great root here." A fortnight afterwards, toward the end of May, Ralegh
was summoned to attend the Council Chamber,
and was told that it was the King's pleasure that
he should resign his office as Captain of the Guard.
The reason given was that the King wished one
of his own countrymen, Sir Thomas Erskine, to
fill this office of trust about his person. To make
up for the loss of this post, a condition attached
to Ralegh's patent as Governor of Jersey, reserving
£300 annually of his salary to the Crown, was
remitted. But the office of Captain of the Guard,
though not profitable, was considered a post of
great honour, and it gave its holder an important
position at Court. Ralegh was bitterly grieved
at losing it, and attributed the loss to Cecil. He
would not seize this opportunity of shaking himself free from Court intrigue, but made a wild
attempt to discredit Cecil in James I.'s eyes. He

wrote the King a letter, in which he threw all the blame of Essex's death upon Cecil, and even went further back, to lay the blame of the execution of Mary Queen of Scots upon Cecil as well as his father.

The authenticity of this letter has been considered doubtful; but the French Ambassador, Beaumont, in a despatch written on May 2nd, says that Ralegh was in such a rage at being dismissed that he went to the King and protested that he would declare to him, and show him in writing, all the intrigues and the stories that Cecil had got up in his prejudice. This statement makes it very likely that Ralegh wrote the letter. But at all events it is certain that he gained nothing by doing so, and probably only excited Cecil's animosity against himself. Ralegh was not the kind of man whom James could have liked under any circumstances. He was too independent, energetic, and impetuous to suit the cautious King. He was as eager as ever for war with Spain, and hoped to make James share his views. At an interview which he had with him at Beddington Park, where James was the guest of Sir Nicholas Carew, Ralegh offered to raise 2,000 men at his own expense and lead them to invade Spanish territory. This sort of talk was very distasteful to James. He had a profound dislike for war; he had won his crown peacefully, and meant to hold it peacefully. It had no doubt been necessary for Elizabeth, whose legitimacy was doubtful, to make war to defend her throne. He, on the contrary, was a legitimate monarch, and his fondest desire was to be recognised as such by all powers, Protestant and Catholic alike. But there was a strong party in England who, like Ralegh, wished him to continue the war with Spain, and above all not to desert the cause of the Netherlands.

Philip II., just before his death, had hoped to make the settlement of affairs in the Netherlands more easy, by giving over his sovereignty there to his eldest daughter Isabella and her husband, the Archduke Albert, a younger brother of the Emperor Rodolph II. But the Netherlanders were no more inclined to submit to the Archdukes, as Isabella and her husband were called, than to the Spanish King himself; for the Archdukes, supported by Spanish troops, were clearly only tools in .the hands of Spain. Ambassadors from the different powers now hastened to the Court of James to congratulate him on his accession, and to gain him, if possible, for their ally.

First came an important embassy from the Dutch Republic; amongst its members was the greatest statesman of the Republic, John of Olden Barneveldt. James answered their demands for alliance with commonplaces, and made no promises. Before the Dutch Embassy had left London, a French ambassador, De Rosny, arrived with a splendid suite of two hundred gentlemen. The special object both of Barneveldt and De Rosny was to obtain such help from James as would prevent Ostend, which was then besieged by Spanish troops, from falling into the hands of Spain. De Rosny wished to bring about a secure alliance between England and France; he proposed a double marriage between the two royal houses; the Dauphin was to marry James's only daughter, Elizabeth, whilst Prince Henry, James's eldest son, was to marry Elizabeth, the eldest daughter of the King of France. James listened, but promised nothing. The children were still young, and he shrank from taking any step which would commit him to any decided course of action. All that could be got from him was a promise to allow the levy of soldiers in England and Scotland for the defence of Ostend.

Cecil, as well as James, seems to have been averse to war with Spain. He cordially disliked Spain; but as a statesman he saw great difficulties in the way of war. England was poor. Elizabeth had always been obliged to use the strictest economy, so as to keep order in financial affairs. The revenue of the Crown was decreasing, and it was clear that the country would not easily bear the burden of war. Financial matters were to be made still more difficult as time went on by the . extravagance of James's Court, and the lavish way in which he spent money on his favourites.

Under these circumstances, Ralegh's talk of war with Spain was very distasteful to James. But

though he met with no favour from the King,
Ralegh still stayed about the Court, hoping
doubtless that some way might appear for him
again to take an active part in affairs.

CHAPTER XI.

Conspiracies against James I.

THE disfavour with which Ralegh was regarded
was shown, amongst other things, by the way
in which he was deprived of his London house.
Durham House was situated in the Strand. It
had originally belonged to the Bishops of Durham,
but had been resigned to the Crown in the time
of Henry VIII. In 1584 Queen Elizabeth had
granted a lease of the house to Ralegh, who spent
much money in repairing it. Immediately on
James I.'s accession, the Bishop of Durham
claimed the house as its rightful owner, and Sir
Walter Ralegh was ordered by royal warrant to
deliver quiet possession of it to him. He was
bidden to clear out with all his goods in a fortnight, a hardship of which he bitterly complained;
for he had stocked the house with provisions for
forty persons, and hay and oats for twenty horses
for the spring. Some years afterwards, in 1608,
on the site of the yard and tumble-down offices
of Durham House, arose a mighty building,
founded at the suggestion of Robert Cecil, and
called the New Exchange. Below were cellars

in which to store goods; and above, a well-paved walk, with rows of shops. The place became a fashionable resort, and is often spoken of in the plays and other writings of the day.

There were many discontented minds in England on the accession of James I., and a plot greeted the new King at the very beginning of his reign. The most striking thing about this plot is its entire futility. The truth is that there was no great cause to struggle for, and only small men tried to find occupation for their restless brains by plotting.

The Catholics had hoped much from the accession of James I., but as yet had obtained nothing. One William Watson, a secular priest, a vain, foolish man, who was chiefly influenced by bitter animosity to the Jesuits, had struggled to make himself the mouthpiece of the Catholic gentry, and gain promises of favour from James. But the King was in no hurry to do anything, and Watson, in his impatience to obtain distinction, began to talk over his grievances with other Catholics. The chief of his confidants were Sir Griffin Markham, a Catholic gentleman, and George Brooke, the younger brother of Lord Cobham, who, though a Protestant, was quite ready to have a share in any mischief. The idea of the conspirators was to gain possession of the King's person, and then obtain from him such promises as they desired.

A number of Catholics were drawn into the

plot, and even Lord Grey de Wilton was persuaded to join it. He was a brave, impetuous
young nobleman, son of Lord Grey de Wilton,
who had been lord-deputy in Ireland when
Ralegh fought there. He was a Puritan, and was
persuaded to join this Catholic plot on the plea
that perfect tolerance was to be extorted from the
King for Catholics and Puritans alike. The plot
never reached any important dimensions. By the
end of June the government was aware of its
existence, and the conspirators fled from London,
but were taken one by one.

The examination of the prisoners brought to
light the existence of another conspiracy, in which
Ralegh's enemies accused him of having a share.
The whole story of this conspiracy is covered with
mystery, and the real truth about it will probably
never be known. Suspicion was at once directed
against Lord Cobham by the fact that his brother
was one of the conspirators in the Catholic plot.
Ralegh was at that time in attendance on the
Court at Windsor Castle. One day in the middle
of July he came out on to the castle terrace ready
to go hunting with the royal party. As he paced
the castle terrace Cecil came to him, and bade him
stay, that he might attend upon the Lords of the
Council Chamber, who wished to ask him some
questions. In answer to these questions, Ralegh
told the Lords of the Council that he knew
nothing of any plot to surprise the King's person,
nor of any plot contrived by Lord Cobham.

Shortly after this Ralegh wrote, first to the Lords of the Council and then to Cecil, saying that he believed Cobham had had dealings with Aremberg, the ambassador who had just come over from the Archduke Albert. From Durham House he had seen Cobham rowed across the river to a house where a well-known agent of Aremberg's, Renzi, lived. This letter of Ralegh's was shown to Cobham, and excited in him violent anger against Ralegh. He thought Ralegh had betrayed him. In reality his brother, George Brooke, had already made known his connection with Aremberg. Writing about this letter afterwards, Ralegh says, "The same was my utter ruin; I did it to do the King service."

Cobham now looked upon Ralegh as his bitter enemy. In his examination he confessed that he had conferred with Aremberg about receiving money from the King of Spain, to be distributed amongst the discontented in England; but he said that his chief instigator in his dealings with Spain had been Sir Walter Ralegh. Immediately after this statement of Cobham's, Ralegh himself was committed to the Tower. Then followed the examination of all the supposed conspirators. It went on through the remainder of July and nearly the whole of August; to try and discover the truth of the matter out of the confused and contradictory answers received is a hopeless task. Both George Brooke and Cobham seem to have answered without any regard to truth. They con-

tradicted themselves and enlarged upon their first
statements in the most reckless manner. To found
any charge against Ralegh upon their statements
would be most unjust. Clearly it was their desire
to ruin him, and, if possible, by accusing others, to
save themselves. It is difficult to discover what
Cobham had really plotted to do. He seems to
have chafed at the supremacy of Cecil and the
Howards with the King, and to have hoped by
some change of government to have the pleasure
of humbling them. He thought of trying to raise
the Lady Arabella Stuart to the throne. He
negotiated with Aremberg before his arrival, and
obtained the promise of money from him. After
Aremberg's arrival he continued his intercourse
with him, and even offered to go to Spain, with
a view of persuading the King of Spain to listen
to his projects. He was accused of having talked
of destroying "the King with all his cubs;" but
this statement George Brooke afterwards denied
on the scaffold.

Suspicions were at first directed against Ralegh
on account of his well-known intimacy with Cobham, as well as by the fact that he was known to
be extremely discontented with the state of affairs
generally, and with the treatment which he had
received. He probably knew more of Cobham's
plottings than he cared to disclose; but there
seems no evidence that he had shared them. He
had been offered some of the money which Aremberg promised Cobham, but had refused it at once.

It is not likely that a man of Ralegh's ability, if he had plotted at all, would have plotted in such a feeble manner as did Cobham.   He may have talked over with him possible courses to take, with a view of recovering power and influence; but, considering the hatred with which he regarded Spain, it is not likely that he would have entered into negotiations with the Spanish Court.   It is well known that the Spaniards always regarded him as their bitterest foe in England.   "God doth know," he says, writing to the Lords of the Council, "that I have spent forty thousand pounds of mine own against that King and nation; . . . . that I have been a violent persecutor and furtherer of all enterprises against that nation. . . . . Alas! to what end should we live in the world, if all the endeavours of so many testimonies shall be blown off with one blast of breath, or be prevented by one man's word."

Confinement, and the accusations which were brought against him, so told upon his health and spirits that, after he had been in the Tower a fortnight, he tried to put an end to his life, but fortunately without success; for he only inflicted a slight wound from which he soon recovered.   In a long letter which he wrote to his wife to bid her farewell, he explained his reasons for this attempted suicide.   " Receive from thy unfortunate husband," he writes, "these his last lines; these the last words that ever thou shalt receive from him, that I can live never to see thee and my child more! I cannot. I have desired God and disputed with my reason, but nature and compassion hath the victory. That I can live to think how you are both left a spoil to my enemies, and that my name shall be a dishonour to my child—I cannot endure the memory thereof. Unfortunate woman, unfortunate child, comfort yourselves; trust God, and be contented with your poor estate! I would have bettered it if I had enjoyed·a few years. Thou art a young woman, and forbear not to marry again. It is now nothing to me; thou art no more mine nor I thine. To witness that thou didst love me once, take care that thou marry not to please sense, but to avoid poverty and to preserve thy child. . . .

"For myself, I am left of all men, that have done good to many. All my good turns are forgotten; all my errors revived and expounded to all extremity of ill. All my services, hazards, and expences for my country—plantings, discoveries, fights, councils, and whatsoever else . . . malice hath now covered over. I am now made an enemy and a traitor by the word of an unworthy man. He hath proclaimed me to be a partaker of his vain imaginations, notwithstanding the whole course of my life hath approved the contrary, as my death shall approve it. Woe, woe, woe be unto him by whose falsehood we are lost! He hath separated us asunder; he hath slain my honour, my fortune; he hath robbed thee of thy husband, thy child of his father, and me of you both. O God, Thou dost know my wrongs! . . . But, my wife, forgive them all as I do. Live humble; for thou hast but a time also. God forgive my Lord Harry; for he was my heavy enemy: and for my Lord Cecil, I thought he would never forsake me in extremity! I would not have done it him, God knows. But do not thou know it; for he must be master of thy child, and may have compassion of him. Be not dismayed that I die in despair of God's mercies. Strive not to dispute it, but assure thyself that God hath not left me nor Satan tempted me. Hope and despair live not together. I know it is forbidden to destroy ourselves; but I trust it is forbidden in this sort, that we destroy not ourselves despairing of God's mercy. The mercy of God is immeasurable; the cogitations of men comprehend it not.

"In the Lord I have ever trusted; and I know that my Redeemer liveth. Far is it from me to be tempted with Satan; I am only tempted with sorrow, whose sharp teeth devour my heart. O God, Thou art goodness itself! Thou canst not but be good to me! O God, Thou art mercy itself! Thou canst not but be merciful to me!"

Then, after a few words about his debts, he goes on: "Oh, intolerable infamy! O God, I cannot resist these thoughts! I cannot live to think how I am derided, to think of the expectations of my enemies, the scorns I shall receive, the cruel words of the lawyers, the infamous taunts and

despites to be made a wonder and a spectacle.
O death, hasten thou unto me, that thou mayest
destroy the memory of these, and lay me up in
dark forgetfulness! O death, destroy my memory,
which is my tormentor; my thoughts and my
life cannot dwell in one body! But do thou
forget me, poor wife, that thou mayest live to
bring up my poor child. . . . I bless my poor
child; and let him know his father was no traitor.
Be bold of my innocence; for God, to whom I
offer life and soul, knows it. And whosoever thou
choose after me, let him be but thy politique
husband. But let my son be thy beloved; for he
is part of me, and I live in him; and the difference
is but in the number and not in the kind. And
the Lord for ever keep thee and them, and give
thee comfort in both worlds."

The Lord Harry mentioned in this letter was
Lord Henry Howard, who, by his secret correspondence with James before Elizabeth's death,
had succeeded in prejudicing the King's mind
against Ralegh. He had ingratiated himself with
James by means of the vilest flattery. He became
an ally of Cecil's, to whom he was recommended
by James; and it seems as if, after his connexion
with Howard, Cecil's feelings towards Ralegh
had steadily grown more hostile. After James's
accession, Howard became a member of the
Council, and was made Earl of Northampton in
1604. He continued to pursue Ralegh with bitter
animosity.

Ralegh speedily recovered from his slight wound. He saw now that his one hope was to succeed in persuading Cobham to retract his false statements regarding him. He managed to have a letter conveyed to Cobham, in which he implored him to speak the truth. This letter was tied round an apple, and thrown through the window into the room in the Tower where Cobham was imprisoned, by Cotterell, an attendant of Ralegh's in the Tower. Cotterel brought back the answer, which Cobham had thrust under his door. In this Cobham said: " I never had conference with you in any treason, nor was I ever moved by you to the things I heretofore accused you of; and, for anything I know, you are as innocent and as clear from any treasons against the King as is any subject living. . . . . God so deal with me, and have mercy on my soul, as this is true."

But even this was not to help Ralegh ; and once more before Ralegh's trial Cobham had withdrawn his retractation, and made new charges against his old friend.

CHAPTER XII.

Ralegh's Trial at Winchester.

A S the plague was at that time raging in
London, it was determined that the trial
of the conspirators should be conducted at Winchester. On the 12th of November Ralegh was
brought out of the Tower to be taken to Winchester, under the charge of Waad, Lieutenant of
the Tower. So great was Ralegh's unpopularity
amongst the citizens that he was greeted as he
passed through the streets by the execrations of
the mob. "It was hob or nob," Waad told Cecil,
"whether or not Ralegh should have been brought
alive through such multitudes of unruly people
as did exclaim against him. . . . . If one hare-
brained fellow amongst the multitudes had begun
to set upon him, as they were very near to do it,
no entreaty or means could have prevailed, the
fury and tumult of the people was so great."
We shall see that in the end Ralegh's misfortunes
taught the people to know him as he really was,
and to reverence him in the days of his fall as
much as they had hated him in the days of his
prosperity.

On the 17th of November Ralegh was placed at the bar at Winchester on a charge of high treason. The trial was conducted before a special commission, in which sat, amongst others, Lord Henry Howard, Cecil, and some other lords; Chief Justice Popham, and three other judges. The prosecution was in the hands of Sir Edward Coke as Attorney-General. He behaved throughout the trial with great asperity and violence to Ralegh; so much so, that he called upon himself the censure even of Cecil.

The trial throughout was conducted in a manner which would now seem utterly unjust. At the present day, in a criminal trial, the accused is considered innocent until he is proved guilty, and he is allowed to choose able counsel to defend him from the accusations brought against him. At that time things were very different. The burden of the proof lay with the accused. He was all along considered guilty, unless he could prove himself innocent; and he was allowed no counsel, but was obliged to answer himself, without any preparation, the charges brought against him.

Sir Walter pleaded "Not guilty." He was asked whether he wished to challenge any of the jury, and answered: "I know none of them, but think them all honest and Christian men. I know my own innocency, and therefore will challenge none. All are indifferent to me. Only this I desire: sickness hath of late weakened me, and my memory was always bad; the points in the indictment are many, and perhaps in the evidence more will be urged. I beseech you therefore, my lords, let me answer the points severally as they are delivered; for I shall not carry them all in my mind to the end."

Coke tried to make objections to this request; but he was partially overruled by the Commissioners. After a few preliminary proceedings, Coke proceeded to make a long and violent speech, in which he summed up the charges against Ralegh. But he introduced besides all sorts of matters relative only to the "Surprising Treason," as it was called, of Watson and Markham, which had nothing to do with the accusations against Ralegh. He was several times interrupted by Ralegh, who asked how he was affected by all this; and at last Ralegh exclaimed: "Your words cannot condemn me; my innocency is my defence. Prove against me any one thing of the many that you have broken, and I will confess all the indictment, and that I am the most horrible traitor that ever lived, and worthy to be crucified with a thousand torments."

Then Coke rejoined furiously: "Nay, I will prove all. Thou art a monster; thou hast an English face, but a Spanish heart. You would have stirred England and Scotland both. You incited the Lord Cobham as soon as Count Aremberg came into England to go to him. The night he went, you supped with the Lord Cobham, and he brought you after supper to Durham House; and then, the same night, by a back way, went with Renzi to Count Aremberg, and got from him a promise of the money. After this it was arranged that the Lord Cobham should go to Spain, and return by Jersey, where you were to meet him to consult about the distribution of the money, because Cobham had not so much policy or wickedness as you. Your intent was to set up the Lady Arabella as titular Queen, and to depose our present rightful King, the lineal descendant of Edward IV. You pretend that this money was to forward the peace with Spain. Your jargon was peace, which meant Spanish invasion and Scottish subversion."

When Coke proceeded to dwell on Cobham's treason, Ralegh interposed: "What is that to me? I do not hear yet that you have spoken one word against me. Here is no treason of mine done. If my Lord Cobham be a traitor, what is that to me?" Then Coke broke out: "All that he did was by thy instigation, thou viper. . . . I will prove thee the rankest traitor in all England." This was more than Ralegh could stand. "No, no, Master Attorney," he replied, "I am no traitor. Whether I live or die, I shall stand as true a subject as ever the King hath. You may call me a 'traitor' at your pleasure; yet it becomes not a man of quality or virtue to do so. But I take comfort in it. It is all you can do; for I do not yet hear that you charge me with any treason."

After this Coke proceeded to bring forward his proofs, which were chiefly the results of Cobham's examination. Ralegh in his answer confessed that he had long suspected Cobham of dealings with Aremberg; but he went on to show how utterly unlikely it was that he should have shared in Cobham's plotting. "It is very strange," he said, "that I at this time should be thought to plot with the Lord Cobham, knowing him a man that hath neither love nor following, and myself at this time having resigned a place of my best . command in an office I had in Cornwall. I was not so bare of sense, but I saw that, if ever this State was strong, it was now that we have the kingdom of Scotland united, whence we were wont to fear all our troubles; Ireland quieted, where our forces were wont to be divided; Denmark assured, whom before we were always wont to have in jealousy; the Low Countries, our nearest neighbour. And instead of a Lady, whom time had surprised, we had now an active King, who would be present at his own businesses. For me at this time to make myself a Robin Hood, a Wat Tyler, a Kett, or a Jack Cade, I was not so mad! I knew the state of Spain well: his weakness, his poorness, his humbleness, at this time. I knew that six times we had repulsed his forces; thrice in Ireland; thrice at sea; once upon our coast; and twice upon his own. Thrice had I served against him myself at sea, wherein for my country's sake I had expended of my own property

forty thousand marks.   I knew that when before-
time he was wont to have forty great sails at the
least in his ports, now he hath not past six or seven.
And for sending to his Indies, he was driven to
have strange vessels—a thing contrary to the insti-
tutions of his ancestors, who straitly forbade that,
even in the case of necessity, they should make
their necessity known to strangers.   I knew that
of twenty-five millions which he had from his
Indies, he had scarce any left.   Nay, I knew his
poorness to be such at this time as that the Jesuits,
his imps, begged at his church-doors.   I knew his
pride so abated that, notwithstanding his former
high terms, he was become glad to congratulate
his Majesty, and send unto him.   Whoso knew
what great assurances he stood upon with other
states for smaller sums, would not think he would
so freely disburse to my Lord Cobham six hundred
thousand crowns! . . . . And to show I am not
'Spanish,' as you term me, at this time I had writ
a treatise to the King's Majesty of the present
state of Spain, and reasons against the peace.
For my inwardness with the Lord Cobham it was
only in matters of private estate, wherein, he
communicating often with me, I lent him my best
advice."

In these eloquent terms Ralegh described the
condition of Spain, and his indignation that anyone should think that he could have changed his
lifelong hatred of the Spaniard for traitorous negotiations with him.   His words are said to have

produced a great effect upon the listeners, who had all come there deeply prejudiced against him. Coke merely repeated his accusations. Then Ralegh demanded to have Cobham brought, that he might speak "face to face." Referring to past statutes, and even to canon law, he demonstrated that there must be at least two witnesses to prove a man guilty of treason; and concluded by again begging that Cobham might be sent for. The lawyers denied that he had any right to demand witnesses to prove his treason, and Coke went on with his proofs. Portions of the confessions of the conspirators in the "Surprising Plot" were read, all pointing vaguely to Ralegh's supposed connection with Cobham. Ralegh continued to press that Cobham should be brought; and Cecil seems to have been anxious that this should be done, if the law allowed it. In fact all along Cecil seems to have wished to see Ralegh treated with justice, and given every chance of proving his innocence, though he himself was fully persuaded of his guilt.

The expression made use of by Brooke, "that the King and his cubs" ought to be destroyed together, was brought up against Ralegh, who exclaimed indignantly, "O barbarous! If they, like unnatural villains, spoke such words, shall I be charged with them? I will not hear it. . . . Do you bring the words of those hellish spiders, Clarke, Watson, and others, against me?" Coke broke out in a rage, "Thou hast a Spanish heart,

and thyself art a spider of hell. For thou con-
fessest the King to be a most sweet and gracious
Prince, and yet thou hast conspired against him."
More evidence which proved nothing was produced. Then the results of the examination of
Keymis, Ralegh's trusted friend, who had been
with him in Guiana, were read. He confessed
that he had taken a message and a letter from
Ralegh to Cobham, when both were in the Tower,
bidding Cobham not be afraid, since one witness
could not hurt him. This Ralegh denied, and by
so doing put himself in the wrong; for it was
clear that Keymis was not likely to have invented
the story. Ralegh professed that the statement
had been extorted from Keymis by the sufferings
arising from his close imprisonment, and by the
threat of the rack. On the whole, however, the
evidence against Ralegh proved nothing. The
most absurd things were dragged in to prove him
guilty; amongst others, the remark of a Portu-
guese sailor at Lisbon, that James would never be
crowned, because before that "his throat will be
cut by Don Ralegh and Don Cobham." In summing up, Serjeant Philips said that the question
for the jury was, who they should believe, Ralegh
or Cobham. It was Ralegh's business to prove
the falsehood of Cobham's accusation, and this he
had not done. Coke said that even though " Cobham had retracted, yet he could not rest nor sleep
till he had confirmed." He then read a letter from
Cobham to the Commissioners, in which Cobham

withdrew his retractation, and repeated his accusations against Ralegh.

The reading of this letter was a great blow to Ralegh, who had not suspected that even Cobham could be guilty of such falsehood; but he produced from his pocket the letter which Cobham had written him in the Tower; this was read aloud by Cecil, though Coke tried to prevent it. Then Ralegh turned to the jury, and said, "Now, my masters, you have heard both. That showed against me is but a voluntary confession. This is under oath and the deepest protestations a man can make. Therefore believe which of these hath the most force." The jury then retired; they were only absent a quarter of an hour, and returned with a verdict of "guilty." Ralegh spoke calmly. "My Lords, the jury have found me guilty. They must do as they are directed. I can say nothing why judgment should not proceed. You see whereof Cobham hath accused me. You remember his protestation that I was never guilty. I desire the King should know the wrong I have been done to since I came hither."

Chief Justice Popham, in passing judgment, was not content with abusing Ralegh for his so-called horrible treasons, but went on to abuse him for the heretical opinions which he was supposed to hold. He concluded by passing sentence of death. Ralegh's bearing remained perfectly dignified to the end. He had so behaved throughout the trial, that many of those who had come to

it full of hostile feelings towards him went away
with changed minds, full of sympathy for a man
whose greatness they could not fail to see.   One
man who was present, writing about it, said "that
when he saw Sir Walter Ralegh first he was so
led with the common hatred that he would have
gone a hundred miles to see him hanged; but ere
they parted he would have gone a thousand to
save his life."   Another says, that "never was a
man so hated and so popular in so short a time."
In after years, even one of the judges who sat on
the bench at the trial said, that "never before was
English justice so injured or so degraded" as
then.   Posterity has agreed with this opinion,
and with one voice pronounced Ralegh innocent.
For the jury it may be said in excuse that probably they were unable to see the enormous difference between two such men as Cobham and
Ralegh.   To them the question was which of the
two they should believe.   The lawyers told them
to believe Cobham, and they obeyed.

The truth of the matter seems to be that
Ralegh had listened to Cobham's talk about his
dealings with Aremberg.   Then, when suddenly
questioned at Windsor, he had thought to put an
end to all suspicion by denying the existence of
any understanding between Cobham and Aremberg.   Afterwards he had seen that the truth
must come out, and had confessed what he knew.
But this contradiction had of course tended to
diminish men's belief in his veracity, and had

helped the lawyers to get his condemnation from the jury.

Ralegh's trial took place on the 17th November. A few days after, Cobham and Grey were both tried, and also convicted of high treason. The persons implicated in the "Surprising Treason" had been tried and condemned before. Early in December, Brooke and the two priests, Clerk and Watson, were executed at Winchester. The King was supposed to be full of hesitation as to the fate of the other condemned persons. He probably never intended that they should be executed; but his timid mind was afraid lest they should know of more treasons than they had confessed. He hoped that perhaps at the hour of death they might be led to confess more. Each, therefore, was made to believe that he was actually to be executed. The 10th of December was fixed for the execution of Markham, Grey, and Cobham; the 13th for the execution of Ralegh.

For a few days Ralegh's wonted courage deserted him. He wrote letters to Cecil, to the Lords of the Council, and to the King, in which he begged for life in terms of abject humility, which were quite unworthy of him. His letter to his wife, written later, is very different in tone. It seems strange to us, when we read it, to think that the man who wrote it could have been generally supposed to be an unbeliever and a scoffer at religion. After deploring that he has been unable to provide for her as he would have wished, he goes on to say : "But God hath prevented all my determinations—the great God that worketh all in all. If you can live free from want, care for no more ; for the rest is but vanity. Love God, and begin betimes to repose yourself on Him ; therein shall you find true and lasting riches and endless comfort. For the rest, when you have travelled and wearied your thoughts on all sorts of worldly cogitations, you shall sit down by sorrow in the end. Teach your son also to serve and fear God while he is young, that the fear of God may grow up in him." He then speaks about various moneys which were owed to him, and adds, "And howsoever, for my soul's health, I beseech you pay all poor men." By this time he repented bitterly for the unworthy way in which he had sued for life. He bids his wife, "Get those letters, if it be possible, which I wrote to the lords, wherein I sued for my life ; but God knows that it was for you and yours that I desired it ; but it is true that I disdain myself for begging it. And know it, dear wife, that your son is the child of a true man, and who in his own respect despiseth death, and all his misshapen and ugly forms. I cannot write much. God knows how hardly I steal this time when all sleep ; and it is time to separate my thoughts from the world. . . . I can write no more. Time and death call me away. The everlasting, infinite, powerful, and inscrutable God— that Almighty God that is goodness itself, mercy itself, the true life and light—keep you and yours,

and have mercy on me, and teach to me to forgive
my persecutors and false accusers, and send us to
meet in his glorious kingdom. My true wife,
farewell. Bless my poor boy; pray for me. My
true God hold you both in his arms.

" Written with the dying hand of some time thy
husband, but now, alas, overthrown !

" Yours that was, but now not my own,

"W. RALEGH."

Lady Ralegh herself was doing all that she could
to save her husband's life. She wrote to Cecil: " If
the grieved tears of an unfortunate woman may
receive any favour, or the unspeakable sorrows of
my dead heart may receive any comfort, then let
my sorrows come before you, which if you truely
knew, I assure myself you would pity me, but
most especially your poor unfortunate friend,
which relyeth wholly on your honourable and
wonted favour." Her mental sufferings seem to
have broken down her health; for she concludes
her letter by saying, " I am not able, I protest
before God, to stand on my trembling legs, otherwise I would have waited now on you, or be
directed wholly by you."

On the 10th of December all was ready for the
execution of Markham, Grey, and Cobham. From
the window of the room where he was confined,
Ralegh could see the scaffold, and watched the
strange scene which went on. Markham had just
made himself ready for the executioner, when
there was a stir in the crowd of bystanders. An

unknown Scotchman had arrived in great haste. He spoke a few words with the sheriff, who then, turning to Markham, told him he was to have two hours' respite, and had him led away.   Next Grey was brought on to the scaffold.   He was a very popular man, and his friends were there in great numbers to give him courage to the last.   He had never demeaned himself by asking for life, and now seemed calm and cheerful.   He made a long prayer, but no confession of importance.   Then again the sheriff approached, said Grey was to have a little respite, and had him also led away.   Cobham next appeared, and the same scene was acted over again.   From him too no new confession was extorted, and he only repeated his former accusations against Ralegh.   He seemed prepared to meet death with boldness and contempt.   Whilst he still remained upon the scaffold Markham and Grey were sent for, and the sheriff then told them that the King had given them their lives; this information was greeted by the spectators with much applause.   Ralegh was also told that he was reprieved ; and then he, Cobham, and Grey were all removed to the Tower.   Markham and some others of the conspirators were ordered to leave the kingdom.

Even before Ralegh's trial his offices of Governor of Jersey, Lord Warden of the Stannaries, and Lieutenant of Cornwall, had been declared forfeited, and had been awarded to others.   Now his wine patent was taken away; and he would probably

have been left destitute but for Cecil's kindly
offices. Cecil seems to have acted the part of
a true friend, and to have earned the gratitude
of both Sir Walter and Lady Ralegh. He saved
Ralegh's manor of Sherborne from confiscation,
though many were eager in their suits for it. Cecil
says there were no fewer than a dozen asking for
it. All that Ralegh lost at present with regard
to it was his life interest. He had executed a
conveyance in the last days of Elizabeth, in which
he made over the estate to his wife and son after
his death. This he trusted would still hold good.
We shall see in the future how his wish to hand
down to his son the beautiful estate, which he
had planted with such care and loved so dearly,
was to be disappointed with all his other hopes.

CHAPTER XIII.

Raleigh in the Tower.

SIR WALTER RALEGH expressed his gratitude to James I. for saving his life, in two
letters, which seem to us unworthy of their writer
on account of the high-flown and exaggerated language in which they are written. But we must
remember that this was the fashion of the day;
and that what appears to us absurd, and almost
revolting, was then looked upon as quite natural.
To Cecil also Ralegh expressed his gratitude, and
added entreaties that he would go on exerting
himself in his favour. "Good my Lord," he writes,
"remember your poor ancient and true friend, that
I perish not here, where health wears away, and
whose short times run fast on in misery only.
Those which plotted to surprise and assail the
person of the King, those that are Papists, are at
liberty. Do not forget me, nor doubt me."

During the first year of his imprisonment he
seems to have still cherished the hope that he
might be allowed to leave the Tower, if not to

enjoy complete liberty. He asked Cecil if he might not be allowed to live at Sherborne; adding, "or if I cannot be allowed so much, I shall be contented to live in Holland, where I shall perchance get some employment in the Indies." He was willing even to be put under the care of some bishop or nobleman, as was then sometimes done with state prisoners. He was in bad health, and was anxious to go to Bath to drink the waters. "God doth know," he writes, "that if I cannot go to Bath this fall, I am undone for my health, and shall be dead or disabled for ever."

But all his hopes were to be disappointed. Cecil had done all he meant to do for him. His policy seems to have been to keep out of the way all such men as he feared might prove dangerous rivals. He bore Ralegh no malice; but he was afraid of his genius, and very likely honestly thought that he might be dangerous to the state. Cecil wished to keep all the chief power of the state in his own hands, and he succeeded in so doing. The King himself submitted to his guidance, and trusted everything to him. Cecil was afraid of all violent measures, and profoundly believed that his own policy was the only true policy. He was afraid of Bacon in the same way that he was afraid of Ralegh; for he did not believe in the schemes of reform which Bacon advocated, and so did his utmost to prevent Bacon from exercising too much influence at Court. If we look at Cecil in this way, we shall easily understand his conduct to Ralegh, and shall not need to suspect him of base motives.

By degrees it became clear to Ralegh that he could hope for no more mercy from the King and Cecil. Once, in March, 1604, he was removed from the Tower for a short period; but only to be taken to the Fleet. This was because King James wished to celebrate Easter by coming with all his Court to a grand bear-baiting at the Tower. To commemorate his visit, he wished to pardon all the prisoners then in the Tower; but in order that Ralegh, Cobham, and Grey might not be included in the general pardon, he had ordered them to be removed to the Fleet during his visit.

Ralegh did not waste the time of his imprisonment in vain regrets; and as he was no longer able to take part in the active work of life, he devoted his energies to study. A great deal of liberty was allowed in most cases to the state prisoners in the Tower. They had their own servants to attend upon them; visitors might come and see them; and they were allowed to take exercise within the enclosure of the Tower.

The mass of buildings known as the Tower covers twelve acres of land. In the centre, in the Inner Ward, stands the White Tower, the oldest part of the building, and adjoining it were the royal apartments, with the royal garden. Here at times the English sovereigns had lived, undisturbed by the neighbourhood of their prisoners. Around the White Tower is a circuit of walls with towers, and in these the state prisoners were lodged. Outside them comes an open space, and then the outer circuit of walls. The tower in which Ralegh was lodged was called the Bloody Tower. The origin of the name is not known, though tradition ascribes it to the fact that in it the boy-king, Edward V., and his brother were murdered. From this tower on one side Ralegh looked over the river, and could watch the boats and shipping as they passed by, and gaze out on the wide expanse of country beyond; behind, he had access into a garden, called the lieutenant's garden; and there was also a pleasant walk along the top of a wall which he used frequently to pace, and which still is called "Ralegh's Walk."

During some part of Ralegh's imprisonment his wife and his son Walter were allowed to be with him. At other times Lady Ralegh lived in a house on Tower Hill, which she had hired so as to be near her husband; and here probably, in the spring of 1605, she gave birth to a second son, who was named Carew. The Tower was not a healthy spot, and the plague which had been ravaging London lingered long within its walls. Ralegh's own health suffered severely, and he wrote to Cecil in 1604, begging that he would remember his "miserable estate, daily in danger of death by the palsy, nightly of suffocation by wasted and obstructed lungs; and now the plague being come at the next door unto me, only the narrow passage of the way between us, my poor child having lien this fourteen days next to a woman with a running plague sore, and but a paper wall between, and whose child is also this Thursday dead of the plague." In spite of the plague, Ralegh had to stay on in his unhealthy prison. It was fortunate for him that he had the garden in which to take exercise. Here he built a small laboratory, and devoted himself to chemical studies. The use of this garden was granted him by Sir George Harvey, then Lieutenant of the Tower, who treated his prisoner with great kindness. Harvey frequently dined with him, and allowed his friends easy access to him. But in 1605 Harvey was succeeded by Sir William Waad, who had no such friendly feelings towards Ralegh. He objected to the notice which Ralegh attracted, for he could be seen by passers-by in the garden, and wrote to Cecil, who was now Earl of Salisbury: "Sir Walter Ralegh hath converted a little hen-house in the garden into a still, where he doth spend his time all the day in his distillations. I desire not to remove him, though I want by that means the garden. . . . If a brick wall were built, it would be more safe and convenient." Waad seemed anxious to make the prisoners feel their position, and in 1607 brought out a new code of ordinances for the government of the Tower, which, though they made no important differences, imposed all kinds of small and vexatious restrictions on the liberty of the prisoners.

Ralegh grew famous as a chemist. The Queen,

Ann of Denmark, believed that she owed her recovery from a dangerous illness to a bottle of cordial sent her by him. The Countess of Beaumont, wife of the French Ambassador, coming to the Tower one day to see the lions which were kept there, saw Ralegh in his garden, and stopped to speak with him, and ask him for the gift of one of his bottles of balsam. Thomas Hariot, the mathematician, was one of Ralegh's most intimate friends. He visited him frequently in the Tower, and no doubt aided him in his scientific studies.

In 1606 Ralegh's health was again worse, and his physician suggested that he should be removed to a little room which he had had built in the garden adjoining his still-house, where he would be warmer and drier than in his damp lodging in the Bloody Tower. Accordingly in this garden-house he spent part of his imprisonment. His sufferings were much increased by the thought of the position into which his wife and children were brought by his misfortunes. His wife did not always show herself a brave woman in the midst of their trials, and seems even to have gone so far as to blame Ralegh for negligence. Once, writing to Cecil, he says: "I shall be made more than weary of life by her crying and bewailing. . . . . She hath already brought her eldest son in one hand, and her sucking child in another, crying out of her and their destruction, charging me with unnatural negligence; and that, having provided for my own life, I am without sense and com-

passion of theirs." But this was only a passing
cloud. On the whole the husband and wife seem
to have clung closely together, and to have been a
source of strength and consolation to one another
through all their trouble.

Ralegh would not submit to be cut off from all
share in the interests of his fellow-countrymen.
He hardly hoped that he would ever again enjoy
power and influence; he knew, he said, writing to
Cecil, "that the best of men are but the spoils of
time, and certain images wherewith fortune useth
to play, kisse them to-day and break them to-
morrow." Fortune was not likely to kiss him
again; but yet a little hope must have dawned
upon him when he saw that Prince Henry, James's
eldest son, as he ripened into manhood, learnt to
appreciate his intellect and court his friendship.

Prince Henry was the brightest hope of the
nation. Full of the vigour and freshness of youth,
he was ready, as Elizabeth had been, to identify
himself with the nation, instead of going against
it as his father so often did. He was full of
sympathy for all that was noble and good, and,
far from being timid like his father, his brave
spirit delighted in military exercises. He was
full of enthusiasm for the English seamen who
had defied the Spanish power in Elizabeth's reign.
Amongst living men, none showed to· so great
perfection as Ralegh the qualities which had led
men to do deeds of bravery for Elizabeth and for
England, and it is easy to understand the ad-

miration which the young Henry felt for him. He was not afraid of openly expressing this admiration at Court. No king but his father, he said, would keep such a bird in a cage. Henry took a special interest in all that had to do with the navy and with shipbuilding. He would go down and himself watch the building of the ships, and take a personal interest in the shipwrights. He asked Ralegh to give him his advice about a ship which he meant to build; and an interesting letter from Ralegh to the Prince exists, in which he tells him all the points to be observed in building a good ship.

Prince Henry also asked Ralegh's advice about a still more important matter, the question of his marriage. In the unsettled state of European politics, the different princes were continually trying to strengthen their position by the marriages of their children. France, England, and Spain were each anxious to secure one another's friendship by marriage treaties, and engaged in endless negotiations for this purpose. This was just the sort of thing that James delighted in; to treat as an equal with the great European monarchs made him feel the grandeur of his position. But there were difficulties in the way both of a marriage with Spain and a marriage with France. The great mass of the English were by no means very friendly to Spain. In 1604 a peace had been concluded with Spain, which, on the whole, left matters as it had found them.

The death of Philip II., in 1598, had greatly altered the attitude and policy of Spain. Philip II. had laboured to obtain supremacy in European affairs, that with him the Catholic faith might triumph. With his view he indulged in schemes which kept Europe in constant anxiety; for none felt themselves safe from his aggressions. His death threw all the power in the state into the hands of a man quite unable to carry on his vast schemes. Philip II.'s son, Philip III., who succeeded him, was of a gentle, timid nature, equally free from either vices or virtues; without particular tastes, without strong passions, with no interest but in religion. He could not be roused even to take an interest in his own marriage; and when his father put before him the portraits of three princesses, one of whom he might choose for his bride, he declined to choose for himself, and only said that "his father's will was his taste." A man of this kind was sure to be ruled by some one, and Philip III. fell entirely under the influence of the Count of Lerma, a courtier whom his father had appointed to attend upon his person. His first order on his accession was that Lerma's signature should be as valid as his own. Everything was left in the hands of Lerma, who watched jealously and anxiously lest any one else should step between him and the King. He allowed only persons whom he knew to be entirely devoted to him to approach Philip III.; he forbade even the Queen to speak with her husband about

state affairs. He filled all the important offices
with his creatures, and exalted his own family to
high positions. Lerma was entirely in favour of
peace; he had no warlike tastes, and the finances
of the country were so exhausted by long years of
war that he saw that peace had become an absolute
necessity. But though he tried to economise by
making peace, he introduced a most extravagant
expenditure at home. He ingratiated himself with
the Spanish grandees by restoring the splendour
of the Court, which Philip II.'s stern and unbend-
ing character had banished. It was under his
influence that the luxury and ceremony of the
Spanish Court reached an exaggerated develop-
ment, and became a model for all other Courts.
On Court festivities, and on the magnificence
with which he surrounded the King, Lerma spent
as much as Philip II. had spent before on war,
so that no order was introduced into finances, and
the real weakness of Spain was unchanged. The
people suffered terrible poverty and misery, whilst
their rulers revelled in unexampled luxury.

Lerma's foreign policy had the result of slowly
diminishing the influence of Spain in European
affairs. Philip II. had struggled to identify his
interests with those of the Empire, which was in
the hands of another branch of his own family.
Charles V. had ruled over the Empire, Spain, and
the Netherlands. He had been succeeded by his
son Philip II. in Spain and the Netherlands; by
his brother Ferdinand in the Empire. The posses-

sions of the House of Austria had been further broken up by the cession of the Spanish Netherlands to the Infanta Isabella. Spain and the Empire together were strong enough to resist all Europe; but Lerma's mind could not grasp great schemes. He did not think of the common interests of the House of Austria. He only wanted peace for Spain; and with this view he tried to form firm alliances with England and with France, and consented to make a treaty with the Dutch Republic, by which he recognized its independence. Lerma hoped to bring about a firm alliance with England by means of a marriage between young Henry and the Infanta; and he tried to win over by Spanish gold the leading men in the English government, and at the English court.

The list of names of those who were in receipt of pensions from Spain includes most of the men who then influenced English affairs. Cecil himself accepted a pension of five thousand crowns. It is difficult to see what can have induced him to do so; and though he accepted Spanish money, he did not let himself be won over to Spanish interests. He wished for peace with Spain; but he wanted no alliance, and no marriage. The discovery of the Gunpowder Plot, in 1606, showed the English how little Spain's friendship was to be trusted; for the conspirators had been in treaty with Spain, and had hoped for aid from her. For a time all talk of a marriage was at an end. The

Spaniards then hoped to bind themselves to France
by marriage alliances. "They offer their Infanta
to everybody," James said scornfully. But Henry
IV. of France was not at all inclined to listen to
the overtures of Lerma. During his whole reign
he had set himself with vigour to resist the power
of the House of Austria. He had fought his
way to the crown of France in the teeth of the
opposition of Philip II., supported by a strong
Catholic party in France. When at last Henry,
feeling that in no other way could he become
King of France, became a Catholic, Philip II.
vainly tried to prevent the Pope from removing
the ban of excommunication which had been
laid upon him. Henry became King, and a
stronger King than there had been in France
for some time. Once more there was a King in
Europe who was able to offer real resistance to
the encroachments of Spain. Henry and his great
minister, the Duke of Sully, who always remained
a Protestant, worked together with one purpose.
They wished to give France the blessing of religious toleration, as far as it was then understood,
and to bring back prosperity to the people by
encouraging industries and agriculture. Abroad
they wished to separate, as far as possible, the
different branches of the House of Austria, which
ruled in Spain, Germany, and the Netherlands, and
by uniting themselves with the smaller powers in
Europe—with the Protestant Princes of Germany,
the Dutch Republic, the Duke of Savoy, and, if

possible, the King of England—to prevent Spain
from proceeding with her schemes of aggrandize-
ment. In foreign politics Henry IV. worked in
perfect accord with Barneveldt, the great Dutch
statesman. He profited, as well as the Dutch
Republic, when Spain was forced to recognize
its independence; for in the Dutch Republic
he gained a certain ally against Spain under all
emergencies.

In 1610 the face of European politics was
changed. Henry IV., who was just preparing to
strike a great blow at the House of Austria, perished
by the hand of an assassin, as he rode in his coach
through the streets of Paris. His son, Louis XIII.,
who succeeded him, was a minor, and the Queen,
Mary dei Medici, was appointed regent. She was
entirely opposed to her husband's views, and had
always wished for the Spanish alliance. The
much-talked-of double marriage with Spain was
concluded under her auspices. The young King
was married to the Iufanta Ann, and the Princess
Elizabeth to the Infante Philip of Spain.

The Infanta was disposed of; but still Spain
was anxious to keep up negotiations with England.
Lerma probably never seriously meant that there
should be a marriage. The religious difficulty
could not be got over; for the Spanish King
would not give his daughter to a heretic, and
there was no chance that Henry would turn
Catholic. All Lerma wanted was, by tempting
James with these hopes of a Spanish marriage, to

prevent a marriage which would be contrary to the interests of Spain. Now when Lerma again offered another Infanta, only six years old, Digby, the English Ambassador in Spain, advised James to listen to him no longer. This was what Salisbury wanted. "The Prince," he said, "could find roses elsewhere; he need not trouble himself about this Spanish olive."

Meanwhile, Ambassadors from the Duke of Savoy proposed that a double marriage should be concluded between the son and daughter of the Duke and the son and daughter of the King of England. Henry asked Ralegh's advice on this point, and Ralegh wrote at his request two discourses—one on a marriage between the Lady Elizabeth and the House of Savoy, and the other on a marriage between Prince Henry and a daughter of Savoy. These discourses are both very interesting to any one who wishes to understand the drift of the politics of the time.

Ralegh objected to any marriage between England and Savoy, because he saw no good that could come to England from it. The Duke of Savoy was a weak Prince, engaged all his lifetime in a struggle to extend his dominions. "There are but two princes," writes Ralegh, "that the King hath cause to look after; to wit, France and Spain." Friendship with France was, in Ralegh's eyes, the important thing to secure. He seems to have seen that the chief power in European politics was slowly passing from Spain to France.

He had always, even in the days when Spain seemed most powerful, perceived her real weakness. "For Spain," he writes, "it is a proverb of their own, that the lion is not so fierce as he is painted. His forces in all parts of the world (but the Low Countries) are far under the fame; and if the late Queen would have believed her men of war, as she did her scribes, we had in her time beaten that great empire in pieces, and made their kings kings of figs and oranges, as in old times. But her Majesty did all by halves, and by petty invasions taught the Spaniard how to defend himself, and to see his own weakness; which, till our attempts taught him, was hardly known to himself." To conclude, Ralegh thought that there was no need to hurry about the marriage of the Prince, who was still very young. "While he is free," he writes, "all have hope; but a great deal of malice will follow us after he is had from those that have been refused." The French Princess was still too young; but it would be better to wait for her. A marriage between England and France would counteract the effect of the marriage between Spain and France. To this view James inclined; and the Prince, though he strongly objected to marriage with a Catholic, was led to favour it by the hope that the Queen-Regent of France might be persuaded to send the Princess over to England to be educated, and perhaps converted.

Meanwhile a marriage which greatly pleased the English people, and Ralegh amongst the number, hàd been arranged for the Lady Elizabeth, James's only daughter. In 1610 a marriage contract had been signed between her and the young Elector of the Palatinate, whose father had been the chief supporter of the Protestants in Germany. At the same time James made a treaty with the Princes of the Protestant Union in Germany. In this way England identified herself with the interests of those who were opposed to Spain, and to the House of Austria. She also bound herself more closely to the Dutch Republic; for the mother of the young Elector was sister to Prince Maurice of Orange, the Stadtholder of the Republic.

On the whole the foreign policy of Salisbury had been crowned with success. He had known the poverty of the country too well to lead it into a war with Spain. Besides this, war with Spain would have been impossible for England at the time, on account of the disturbed state of Ireland, where the rebels would gladly have made common cause with Spain. So Salisbury secured for England the advantage of peace. At the same time, by refusing to conclude a definite alliance with Spain, he kept Spain from feeling sufficiently strong to crush the Dutch Republic; and Spain was brought at last to acknowledge the independence of that Republic. Meanwhile the ties which bound England to France were strengthened, at least as long as Henry IV. lived, by common support granted to the Protestant cause in Germany.

At the beginning of his reign James had hoped

that, without regard to religious considerations, he might form intimate relations with the great powers of Europe. But circumstances were too strong for him; the time had not yet come when religious and political interests could be separated. James found that he was compelled to form ties of friendship with the Protestant princes of Europe rather than with Spain. In all this he was greatly led by Salisbury, who, as his father had done before him, wished that England should put herself at the head of Protestant Europe.

But Salisbury did not live to see the marriage of the Lady Elizabeth. His health broke down in consequence of his ceaseless labours, and he died at Marlborough, on his way from Bath to London, in May, 1612, at the early age of forty-nine. There was little mourning at his death. The King was weary of his yoke; the people looked upon him as the cause of the impositions with which they were burdened; the officials of the government and the courtiers hoped for advancement, and liberty to do as they liked. Even Ralegh in his prison must have allowed himself to hope that a change in the government might bring some improvement in his condition. But that same year he lost his best friend. Full of youthful vigour, Prince Henry took no care of his health. He was stricken with a fever in the end of October, and died on the 6th of November. The Queen, in her despair at seeing him in his dying condition, sent to Ralegh to ask if he could do nothing for him. Ralegh sent a bottle of cordial, saying that it was certain to be useful against anything but poison. The Prince drank the cordial and rallied slightly, but soon after passed away. His last conscious words were, "Where is my dear sister?" He had loved her fondly; and now in his last hours she was kept away from his bedside for fear of infection. It is said that in desire to get to him she disguised herself as a man, and so tried, though in vain, to penetrate into his room.

The people mourned bitterly over their beloved Prince. They fancied he must have been poisoned. Dark suspicions were cherished against different men about the Court, and these were even shared by the Queen. Ralegh's hopes of favour through the friendship of the Prince were at an end. The Queen seems still to have remained his friend, but could do nothing for him. He had addressed her a letter before, asking her to exert herself to obtain his liberation, that he might assist in the plantation of his former colony of Virginia. He must have heard with interest of the new attempt, in 1606, to plant this colony, and of the difficulties through which it had to struggle, till at last, in 1611, it was placed on a secure footing. He must have longed to be able to aid in carrying on the work which he had first started. "I do still humbly beseech your Majesty," he writes to Queen Ann, "that I may rather die in serving the King and my country than to perish here."

Neither did he lose any of his interest in Guiana. In 1606 and 1608, voyages had been made thither by Captains Leigh and Harcourt, who found that the natives still remembered Ralegh, and spoke of him with affection. Ralegh tried by letters and otherwise to entice Cecil, the Queen, or the Lords of the Council, to take an interest in Guiana, telling them of the rich mines of gold which were to be found there, and of the fabulous resources of the country. In 1611 there seems to have been some talk of Keymis undertaking a voyage to Guiana. The plan apparently was that Keymis was to go to Guiana at the expense of the government; but if he failed to bring back half a ton of gold ore, all the charges of the voyage were to be laid upon Ralegh. If Keymis brought back the gold ore, Ralegh was to be set at liberty. In a letter of Ralegh's to the Lords of the Council on this subject, he speaks of the existence of a Spanish settlement —St. Thome—near the mine, and discusses the number of men which would be necessary to secure the safe passage of the English to the mine. This voyage of Keymis never came off; but we do not know what prevented it.

After Salisbury's death the government fell almost entirely into the hands of favourites. James had attached himself with extravagant fondness to a young Scot, by name Robert Carr, on account of his cheerful disposition and fine person. He lavished gifts upon him, and would refuse him

nothing. In 1608 Carr, who wished to become a
landed proprietor, cast longing eyes on Ralegh's
estate of Sherborne. A flaw in the conveyance
of the estate to Ralegh's son gave James some
show of legal right in seizing it. No entreaties
could move the King. Lady Ralegh, leading her
two sons by the hand, threw herself at his feet,
and begged for mercy; but the only answer she
got was, "I maun have the land; I maun have it
for Carr." Ralegh wrote a letter of entreaty to
Carr himself. "For yourself, sir," he wrote,
"seeing your day is but now in the dawn, and
mine come to the evening, ... I beseech you
not to begin your first buildings upon the ruins
of the innocent, and that their griefs and sorrows
do not attend your first plantation." But this
too was without effect; and in 1609 the manor
was granted to Carr. As compensation, a sum of
£8,000 in ready money was given to Raleigh, and
a pension of £400 a year granted to Lady Ralegh,
to be paid during her own lifetime and that of
her eldest son. This was a good deal below the
value of the estate. We know that shortly afterwards Carr sold it back to the King for £20,000.

In 1611 Carr was made Viscount of Rochester.
After Salisbury's death, when James became his
own secretary, he used to settle most of the
affairs of State in consultation with Rochester.
He was strengthened in this course of conduct
by the discovery made in 1613 by Digby, his ambassador in Spain, of a list of the Englishmen in

receipt of Spanish pay. Great was the horror of
James and Digby when they discovered on this
list the names of most of the Privy Councillors,
and of Salisbury himself; but Rochester's name
was not there. The result naturally followed that
James lost all confidence in his councillors, and
clung more than ever to his favourite, whom he
thought he could bind closely to himself by personal favours. By degrees power slipped away
from the hands of the members of council, and
the management of affairs was left in James's
hands. Not much good came to the nation from
the contrivances of James and Rochester, neither
of whom were capable of noble aims or a disin-
terested policy. Their policy seemed to be made
up of petty intrigues, miserable contrivances, and
small oppressions, which daily put James more
and more out of sympathy with the people he
was called upon to rule.

Bacon's position with regard to James is hard
to understand. His was a mind which was ever
planning wide and searching schemes of reform.
These he thought could only be carried out by
the King, aided by the advice of the Lords of the
Council. For such a work he thought Parliament
totally unfit. His temper of mind led him to
admire greatly the prerogative. The sovereign
placed in an irresponsible position must be the
best instrument for carrying out those plans of
reform which seemed needful for the good of the
nation. So it came about that he shut his eyes

to the pettiness of James's aims, and lent himself
to aid him in many of his mean and miserable
contrivances.   He was ambitious of power and
wealth for himself, and he hoped to gain these by
serving James.   He was blind to the temper of
the times; and instead of aiding the cause of the
people, the true cause of reform, lent his great
intellect to patch up the government of James
and his favourites.

CHAPTER XIV.

The History of the World.

RALEGH'S discourses about the marriages of the Prince of Wales and the Lady Elizabeth show with what interest and attention he followed the politics of the day, and made himself completely master of them. He seems to have interested himself more in foreign politics than in the religious questions which occupied people's minds at home. Perhaps it was because he did not take up with zeal the side either of the Puritans or the Episcopalians that he was so generally credited with being an unbeliever in religion. In his writings he shows himself a sincerely religious man; but in the state of religious feeling at the time no place was allowed to the tolerant man—every one was forced to be a partisan.

Ralegh's political knowledge is shown in other tracts besides those about the marriages. One, *Touching a War with Spain*, is chiefly concerned with his favourite theme, the weakness of the Spanish monarchy. *Maxims of State* and the *Cabinet Council*, two treatises on statecraft, are

interesting as showing the influence which the
study of Machiavelli's writings had had upon
him.   Though he repeatedly disclaims Machiavelli's conclusions, we cannot fail to see how he
had gained in acuteness and political wisdom
from the study of the writings of that large-
minded political theorist.   The *Maxims of State*
is particularly interesting from this point of view,
and is full of pithy and pointed sayings; others
of his tracts are concerned with questions relating to the navy and shipbuilding.   But Ralegh
in prison could hardly follow the course which
English politics were taking.   Parliament was
becoming a very different thing from what he
had known it to be in the days of Elizabeth.
He had no idea of the hostile feelings with which
James and his Parliament regarded one another.
In a treatise called *A Discourse on the Prerogative
of Parliament*, published in 1615, he discussed
the King's financial proceedings, and bade him
improve his position by leaving off all his unpopular ways of raising money, and casting himself upon the love of his subjects.   James could
not stand criticism of his government.   It is true
that Ralegh threw all the blame upon the evil
councillors whom he thought had misled the King;
but James knew, if Ralegh did not, how entirely
all that had happened was his own doing.   If
Ralegh had better understood the position of
affairs he would never have hoped to gain favour
by sending this treatise to the King.

Writing political tracts however was not Ralegh's main occupation in the Tower. He had thrown himself heart and soul into study, and had conceived the ambitious design of writing a history of the world. He had grasped the idea of the unity of history, and wishing to write a history of his own country, thought that it could not be rightly comprehended unless it were prefaced by a history of the whole world. Men were beginning at this time really to interest themselves in historical study. The early chroniclers had contented themselves with repeating the facts of early history, as others had told them before, without any attempt at arrangement or criticism, and had then passed on to tell the events which had happened in their own lifetime. A change was now beginning, and England possessed a few real and careful students of history, who, following the example of learned men on the Continent, were trying to master their subject and produce thoughtful and accurate works.

Chief among these was William Camden, who passed his life first as second master, and afterwards as head master, of Westminster School. He was a real scholar and student, and the fame of his learning reached to the Continent, and brought him into connexion with foreign scholars. In 1640 he published his first great work, the *Reliquæ Britannicæ*, in which he described the countries of England, Ireland, and Scotland. Respect for his learning and the purity of his life made Burleigh

fix upon him as the man most fitted to write an
account of the reign of Elizabeth. He gave him
for this purpose a large number of state papers;
and eighteen years afterwards, in 1615, Camden
published his *Annals of England during the Reign
of Elizabeth*. The book was written in Latin, but
was translated soon after. It is written with as
much impartiality as can be expected from a
historian of his own times, and is a valuable
contribution to our knowledge of those days.

Students were also beginning to interest themselves in the history of other countries besides
their own. In 1610 a *General History of the Turks*
appeared, by Richard Knolles, who had been a
fellow of Lincoln College, Oxford. He wrote in
English, with spirit and vigour, and told the story
of the growth of the Turkish Empire, from the
first appearance of the Turks in Europe down to
his own times.

All over Europe the enthusiasm for study, for
learning for its own sake, was advancing. Men
like Isaac Casaubon in France, and the Scaligers
in Belgium, devoted themselves to the study of
classical authors, with a view of obtaining correct
texts. In England scholars like Sir Robert Cotton
were busy collecting literary materials, which had
been scattered by the dissolution of the monasteries,
that others might make use of them. In 1602
Sir Thomas Bodley had conferred an inestimable
boon upon students by the foundation in Oxford
of that great library which has since been known

by his name. Amongst the questions which men then studied, there were many that seem to us absurd and worthless. They busied themselves with points of rabbinical lore, with the exact position of the garden of Eden, with the wanderings of Cain, with discussions as to the spot on which the Ark rested. Long dissertations on points such as these tend to make the first portions of Ralegh's *History of the World* wearisome reading. The story advances so slowly, the questions discussed are so entirely wanting in interest to the modern reader, that neither beauty of style nor the presence here and there of deep and thoughtful sayings, can make it attractive reading. Ralegh was aided, particularly in the scriptural part of his history, by other learned men. He was in continual intercourse with the scholars of his time. Chief amongst those who helped him was one Dr. Robert Burhill, a learned clergyman. We find him also writing to Sir Robert Cotton for the loan of books and manuscripts.

To us the interest of the book does not rest upon this kind of learning, though it is another sign of the wonderful many-sidedness of Ralegh, that he who shone so in active life as soldier, sailor, and statesman, should have been able when in prison to throw himself into study of this occult kind. It was late in life for him to undertake a work on so large a scale; and it is no wonder that the book was never finished. The six volumes which exist only bring the history

down to B.C. 170. Ralegh himself was well aware
how hopeless a task he was undertaking, and
states in his preface his deep feeling of his own
unworthiness for it. "But," he says, "those in-
most and soul-piercing wounds, which are ever
aching while uncured, with the desire to satisfy
those few friends which I have tried by the fire
of adversity—the former enforcing, the latter persuading—have caused me to make my thoughts
legible, and myself the subject of every opinion,
wise or weak." In Ralegh's eyes the great
advantage of the study of history was the moral
instruction which might be got from it. "In a
word," he says, "we may gather out of history
a policy no less wise than eternal, by the com-
parison and application of other men's forepast
miseries with our own like errors and ill-deserv-
ings." It is true that in this way much may be
learnt from the study of history; but it is the
part of the moral teacher rather than of the
historian to point out these lessons. Ralegh
confuses the two functions, and is too much of
a preacher to be a historian. It is not from a
historical but from a literary point of view
that we must judge his book. It holds a foremost place amongst the English prose writings of
the time. Till the days of Elizabeth all learned
books had been written in Latin; and since the
days of Wiclif there had been no great prose-
writer. But with the revival of poetry, prose
began to revive also. At first it was elaborate

and artificial. A style both of speaking and writing came into vogue, by which men seemed to strive to conceal their meaning by the fanciful language in which they clothed it. This affectation was called euphuism, after the novel of *Euphues*, by John Lyly, which is one of the chief though not one of the worst examples of this style. Sir Philip Sydney did not escape the general taint. His pastoral romance called the *Arcadia* is for the most part written in a fanciful and affected manner, but is at the same time full of true poetical feeling. In his *Defence of Poesy* he shows himself master of a purer and freer style. This essay is the most remarkable prose-writing of the Elizabethan age; it is the beginning of literary criticism. Graceful and easy, full of witty and pointed sayings, it shows a remarkable advance on anything that had gone before. Then followed Hooker with his *Ecclesiastical Polity*, the first books of which were published in 1594. He shows how the English language may be used for purposes of argument and scholarly reasoning; and his style is forcible and unaffected, rising at times into nervous eloquence. But no work shows so well the advance both in learning and in prose-writing as the English Bible.

The work of translating the Bible was begun in 1607, and was finished in 1611. It was the labour of forty-seven men, who divided themselves into six companies, and met at Oxford, Cambridge, and Westminster. The work of each person was submitted to the rest for criticism. Such high excellence of style, combining perfect simplicity and true poetry with rare vigour and dignity, exists in no other English book ; and as the Bible was in every one's hands, it produced an effect upon both the spoken and written language which no other book could have done.

It was in 1614 that Ralegh published his *History of the World*. As has been said, it is to its literary merits that the book owes its main value. The language is pure and dignified. The sentences may sometimes strike us as long and cumbersome, but they are in the main easy and flowing, and impress the ear with a feeling of completeness. Occasionally he rises to real eloquence, especially when describing battles. His account of the Punic War is one of the most striking parts of the book. It is when he is dealing with men and their doings that he is at his best; it is then that we seem to see Ralegh's real character much more than when he indulges in philosophical speculations.

To illustrate events in the history of the bygone world, he makes digressions about things which happened in his own time ; and these, being often the accounts of personal experiences, are of great interest, from the light which they throw upon the character of their writer and of his doings. They make us regret very much that he was not able to bring down his history to his own times. No man could have written a more stirring

account of the great events in which he had taken
part.

Ralegh had hoped that this book might win
him favour from James I.; but this hope showed
how little he understood James's views about the
dignity of kings. In his preface Ralegh spoke
of the different English kings, and traced the
misfortunes of many of them to their own evil
doings; above all, he spoke severely of Henry
VIII. James thought that a king was above
criticism; and that any one should presume to
find fault with his own ancestor was unpardon-
able presumption. When asked why he did not
like Ralegh's *History*, he replied, "It is too
saucy in censuring the acts of princes." Other
men judged differently. A greater man than James,
Oliver Cromwell, writing to his son Richard, in
1650, says, "Recreate yourself with Sir Walter
Ralegh's *History* ; it is a body of history, and will
add much more to your understanding than frag-
ments of story." In the century after the first
appearance of this book eleven editions of it were
sold, so great was its popularity. But Ralegh
never published any more, though he seems to
have been far on in his preparation of other
portions. Other things came in to occupy his
attention, and to turn his mind once more to the
business of active life. Distress at the death of
Prince Henry is also said to have left him without courage to resume his writing.

Ralegh's literary labours brought him into con-

P

nexion not only with the learned men of his day,
but also with the men of letters. Besides being
a scholar, he was also a poet, and as such seems
to have been on intimate terms with the great
poets and dramatists of those times. He founded
a club, in a tavern called "The Mermaid," by
Cheapside, at which Shakspeare, Ben Jonson,
Beaumont, Fletcher, and others met and made
merry. Of the meetings at "The Mermaid"
Beaumont speaks in a letter to Jonson from the
country—

> " What things have we seen
> Done at the Mermaid, heard words that have been
> So nimble and so full of noble flame
> As if that everyone from whom they came
> Had meant to put his whole wit in a jest."

Ralegh kept up his intimacy with Ben Jonson
whilst he was in prison. Jonson is said to have
aided Ralegh in his *History*, and in 1613 he
travelled on the Continent with Ralegh's eldest
son.

Ralegh himself was a poet; and those poems of
his that remain are again a proof of the fulness
and manysidedness of his active nature. His
poems for the most part appeared in two col-
lections of English poetry, one of which, called
England's Helicon, was published in 1600, and the
other, *Davidson's Rhapsody*, in 1602. They are
mostly amorous and pastoral lays and sonnets of
the kind that were common in those days. One of
a very different kind, called *The Lie*, is a bitter

and powerful satire upon the existing state of things.   In it he exclaims against the powers that ruled in England at that time—

> " Go, tell the court it glows
>   And shines like rotten wood ;
> Go, tell the church it shews
>   What's good, but does no good.
>   If court and church reply,
>   Give court and church the lie.
>
> "Tell potentates they live
>   Acting by others actions !
> Not lov'd, unless they give ;
>   Not strong but by their factions.
>   If potentates reply,
>   Give potentates the lie."

CHAPTER XV.

Ralegh's last Voyage.

THE result of Cecil's foreign policy had been to place James at the head of the Protestant party in Europe. In 1613 it had even seemed possible that war between England and Spain would once more break out. The Spaniards were so alarmed by the attitude of the English that the Spanish ambassador in London was recalled, in order that an abler man might be put in his place. The man chosen, Diego Sarmiento de Acuna, afterwards known as the Count of Gondomar, was admirably suited for the purpose. He was deeply impressed with the importance of the task entrusted to him, and put his whole heart into it. He found the King anxious for a marriage between his son Charles and a French Princess; but he did not despair of bringing back James in time to a Spanish marriage. Circumstances favoured him. The Parliament summoned in 1614 had shown itself unwilling to listen to the King's demands. James had dissolved it in disgust. He was in great want of money, and this helped to make him turn to Spain once more. The Infanta would bring with her a larger dowry than could the French Princess. He thought that if he had the King of Spain as his

firm friend, he should be enabled to do without
Parliament. Sarmiento was only too ready to welcome James's approaches. He saw that a great
struggle between the Protestant powers and the
Catholic powers was drawing near ; and he believed
that if England could be drawn away from the
Protestants, their party would fall to pieces. Negotiations were entered into with Spain for the
marriage. At first the Spanish demands were such
that even James felt it was impossible to agree to
them. But Digby, the English ambassador at
Madrid, succeeded in bringing about some slight
modifications. He was not in favour of the marriage ; but after protesting against it to James, he
had agreed to undertake the charge of the negotiations. James, when he had received the modified
demands, still hesitated ; and the opponents of
Spain in the English Council determined to do
their utmost, while the hesitation still lasted, to
make the marriage impossible.

Chief amongst these was Sir Ralph Winwood,
now secretary. He had been for some years ambassador at the Hague, and was devoted to the Protestant cause, and entirely opposed to Spain. He
turned for support in his views to the man who was
the embodiment of the spirit of hostility to Spain,
the man in whom still breathed the soul of the
heroes of Elizabeth's days—Sir Walter Ralegh.

Ralegh had often spoken to Winwood of the
advantages which might be gained from the colonization of Guiana. It was his darling scheme; and

he knew that it was a certain way of striking a blow at Spain. He was convinced, from what he had heard whilst in Guiana, that there was a gold mine there which might be made a permanent source of riches to the King. Later times have shown the correctness of his assertions, which at first, after the failure of his expedition, were almost universally disbelieved. Gold is now worked on a large scale in a place called the Caretal Gold Field, in the very region where Ralegh expected so confidently to discover a rich gold mine. His tales of possible gold were very attractive to the ears of Villiers, the King's new favourite. Rochester had fallen from his high position; he was a prisoner in the Tower on a charge of murder. He had been succeeded in the King's favour by Sir George Villiers, who, like Rochester, had attracted James by his fine person and cheerful disposition. Villiers and Winwood both did their utmost to persuade the King to set Ralegh free, and allow him to make an expedition to Guiana.

It is strange that James should have listened to them, just when he was entering into close negotiations with Spain. It seems as if he had hoped to lessen Winwood's objection to the Spanish marriage by allowing him to have his way in this matter at least. On the 19th March, 1616, a warrant was sent to the Lieutenant of the Tower, bidding him to allow Ralegh to go free, under the care of a keeper, to make preparations for his voyage.

No pardon was granted to Ralegh; his future

was to depend solely on his finding the mine. He went out of the Tower with the sentence of death still hanging over his head. It is no wonder that, after his twelve years of prison-life, he eagerly seized any opportunity that offered itself of sharing once more the joys and perils of active life. But the chances of success were small indeed. According to the commission given him for his voyage, he was only to visit such lands as were possessed and inhabited by heathen people. James wished it to be clearly understood that he authorised no interference with Spanish subjects. To make this still more clear, Ralegh was called upon to undertake that he would not hurt any subject of the King of Spain. James was willing enough to have the gold, but he would not do anything which could give the Spaniards any ground of complaint against him. Ralegh must have clearly seen how impossible it would be for him to find the mine on these terms, seeing that Guiana was already in part colonized by Spain. Winwood no doubt hoped that the expedition might tend to bring about a breach with Spain. Ralegh himself spoke to Bacon, perhaps in bravado, about seizing the Mexican fleet; and when Bacon exclaimed, "But that would be piracy," answered, "O no; did you ever hear of men who are pirates for millions? They who aim at small things are pirates." Besides the likelihood of dangerous consequences, the expedition was unwise from another point of view. The colony in Virginia had only just succeeded in establishing

itself. It would have been well if English colonizing efforts had been directed for the time only to
the Northern Continent of America, where there
was enough to do, and had left the Southern Continent to Spain.   James's conduct in allowing the
expedition, the possible consequences of which he
did not trouble himself to consider, is unpardon-
able.   For Ralegh it may at least be said, that he
had everything to gain and little to lose.

Sarmiento had heard with alarm of the proposed
expedition.   He looked upon it as a clear act of
aggression upon Spain, and protested against it
vehemently.   He believed that once upon the seas
Ralegh would be sure to turn pirate.   If Ralegh
really wished to go to Guinea, he said that the
king of Spain would gladly send some ships to
escort him there, and would let him bring back as
much gold and silver as he needed.   But to this
Ralegh could not agree.   James did his utmost to
pacify Sarmiento by promising that the voyage
should lead to no breach with Spain, and consoled
himself by thinking that at least he had no responsibility in the matter.

The preparations for the expedition went rapidly
forward.   Ralegh prepared to venture his all on it.
He spent upon it the £8,000 which he had received
from the King in part payment for the Sherborne
estate, and his wife sold some property of hers
near Mitcham to raise more money.   They must
have been hopeful of success to be thus prepared
to risk everything on the venture.   Others were

willing to embark their money on the expedition,
tempted by the promises of gold or the prospects
of successful colonization. A fine new ship called
the *Destiny* was built for Ralegh. The expedition
altogether numbered twelve vessels, two fly-boats,
and a caravel; of these, the *Destiny*, of 440 tons
burden, was far the largest. She was built in the
Thames, and when completed lay there with most
of the other ships whilst the final preparations
were made.

The fleet attracted much attention, and was
visited by all the principal persons about the
town and Court. Amongst others, the French
ambassador, Desmarets, came to see the ships.
He met Ralegh accidentally on board, and had
some talk with him. In reporting this talk to
his government, he said that " Ralegh had spoken
with bitter discontent of the treatment which he
had received, and had promised, on his return, to
leave his country, and make the king of France
the first offer of whatever might fall under his
power." The fact that Desmarets did not report
this conversation till a month after it had taken
place tends rather to make us distrust his statements. If Ralegh had really said anything so important Desmarets would surely have reported it
at once. But it is beyond doubt that Ralegh was
in communication with Montmorency, the admiral
of France, and had asked him to get permission
from Lewis XIII. for him to take refuge in a
French port when he came back. The man through

whom these communications were made was a certain Captain Faige. From documents which have lately been discovered at Simancas, it appears that Faige and another Frenchman, Belle, were to join Ralegh and his fleet off the Isle of Wight with two ships, and to aid him in an attack upon the Mexican fleet, the profit of which was to be shared by the French. The authority for this is a voluntary statement, made by Belle, at Madrid, in 1618. The Frenchmen did not join Ralegh, according to Belle, "because they did not wish to go with people who were Huguenots."

Almost at the last moment an attempt was made to divert Ralegh's expedition to another purpose. The ambassador of the Duke of Savoy was in London, asking once more for assistance from James for his master. He suggested to Ralegh how easy it would be for him, if a few of the King's vessels were added to his fleet, to seize Genoa, a port which the Duke of Savoy had long coveted. Genoa was then a rich community of money-lenders, from whom Spain largely drew her supplies. The fact that this would be an easy way of striking a blow at Spain made Ralegh willingly listen to the Ambassador's proposals. Even James seems to have entertained the idea for a moment; but it was put a stop to by the conclusion of a definite peace between Spain and Savoy.

Sarmiento tried once more to stop the expedition altogether. James said that it was out of

his power to do so, but that he would put the
case before the council. When the council met,
Ralegh's friends came in force, and overruled
all objections to the expedition. Winwood was
bidden to bear a letter to Sarmiento from Ralegh,
in which Ralegh stated that he meant to make no
attack upon the subjects of the king of Spain.
At the same time a list of the vessels which took
part in the expedition was given to Sarmiento.
Some weeks before, warnings of the possible
coming of Ralegh had been sent out from Madrid
to the Indies; and these were afterwards repeated
in a more pressing form. Prospects were not very
hopeful for Ralegh. In the commission given
him by the King the customary words implying
the royal grace and favour had been carefully
erased, so that the granting of the commission
might not constitute a pardon; and he was said
to be under the peril of the law. He was sixty-
three years old—too old to face the perils and
hardships of such an expedition. But his courage
and energy were as great as ever, and he went
forth to do what he could, though the way must
have seemed dark and stormy before him. Even
during the very days of his final preparations,
James was entering into closer relations with
Spain, and was preparing to lay the formal proposals for the marriage before a special body of
commissioners.

Early in April, 1617, Ralegh sailed out of the
Thames with seven of the vessels of his little fleet;

the remainder met him at Plymouth.   On board
his own ship was his eldest son Walter, as captain.
Young Walter was then in his twenty-fourth year,
a bold, open-hearted youth.   He had been sent to
Oxford in his fourteenth year, and his father had
taken care that his studies should be superin-
tended by an able and learned man.   He had
chosen for his tutor Dr. Daniel Fairclough, or
Featley, as he was more generally called, a fellow
of Corpus Christi College, Oxford.   Young Walter
had another tutor, by name Hooker, of a Devonshire family, for ordinary purposes, and so was
well looked after.   Sir Walter himself wrote at
length to Featley on the subject of his son's
training.   Featley says of his views on the subject, that "they show themselves to proceed from
an excellent temper of wisdom, and of love to
his son."

Young Walter seems to have played many
pranks, and given his tutor some trouble.   After
he left Oxford he killed a man in a duel in
London, and was obliged to leave England for a
time.   He went on the Continent, and it is then
that he is supposed to have travelled with Ben
Jonson, who was abroad at the time.   Tradition
says that in London too for a time Walter was
under the charge of Ben Jonson; for a story is told
of his having once, when Ben Jonson had been
partaking too freely of fine old Canary, wheeled
him in a wheelbarrow into his father's presence,
and asked that his tutor might have a lesson in

sobriety. The son seems to have had his father's brave energetic spirit, and must have felt full of eager expectation in starting on his first voyage of discovery.

One of Ralegh's ships was commanded by his old and faithful friend Keymis, on whose testimony the belief in the existence of the mine rested. There had been some difficulty in getting the crews together; the men who had joined were far from being all that Ralegh could have wished, and their character added greatly to the difficulties of the expedition.

The orders which Ralegh issued to the commanders of his fleet on the 3rd of May are an admirable proof of his wisdom, and show at what perfection of order and discipline he aimed. In every ship divine service was to be read morning and night, all swearing was to be punished, gambling was forbidden, complete obedience to superiors was to be enforced, all Indians were to be treated with kindness and courtesy. Rules were also laid down with a view to preserving good health amongst the men; and elaborate regulations were made for the management of the fleet. They at first met with much contrary weather, which delayed them considerably. One vessel was lost, two others were compelled to put back, and the whole fleet was obliged to put into Cork to recruit. At last, on the 6th September, they reached Lancerota, in the Canaries. The inhabitants saw them approach with alarm. They took

the English for the Algerine pirates, who then
ravaged the Mediterranean, and the coasts of
Spain and Africa.   Ralegh entered intó correspondence with the Governor, hoping to buy
provisions from him.   In spite of the Governor's
promises, they waited in vain.   "For mine own
part," says Ralegh, in his diary, "I never gave
faith to his words; for I knew he sought to gain
time to carry the goods of the town, being seven
miles from us, into the mountain."   In the meanwhile three English sailors were killed in chance
skirmishes by the Spaniards, who persisted in
looking upon them as Turks; but Ralegh stead-
fastly refused to break the peace by revenging
their death, and at last went on to Gomera, a town
on the Great Canary, to get the water and provisions of which he stood in need.   Here he fared
better.   The wife of the Governor was of English
descent; and in sending letters to her husband,
Ralegh sent a present to her of "six exceeding fine
handkerchiefs, and six pairs of gloves," writing at
the same time, that "if there were anything in his
fleet worthy of her she should command it."   She
sent back answer that she was sorry her barren
island had nothing worthy of the Admiral; and
sent with her letter four great loaves of sugar,
baskets of lemons, oranges, grapes, pomegranates,
and figs, which Ralegh says were more welcome to
him than one thousand crowns could have been.
Fresh fruit was just what he needed for his sick
men.   To show his gratitude to the lady, he sent

her "two ounces of ambergris, an ounce of extract of amber, a great glass of rose-water, a very excellent picture of Mary Magdalene, and a cut-work ruff." This produced more presents from the lady; hens and more fruit. Meanwhile the vessels were taking in water, which was done, says Ralegh, "without any offence given or received to the value of a farthing." The Governor was so satisfied with their behaviour that he sent Ralegh a letter for Sarmiento, stating how nobly they had behaved.

Misfortunes were already crowding upon Ralegh. At Lancerota he had been deserted by one of his ships, under the command of Captain Bailey, who returned to England. Sickness was rife amongst his men; and his diary contains little but the melancholy record of one death after another. They were overtaken by storms, and beaten about amongst the Cape Verd Islands; one ship was lost, and others were damaged. One after another the men were struck down, and it seemed as if the best and ablest were fated to die.

At last Ralegh himself fell ill. He caught a severe cold from being suddenly called from his bed by a violent storm. For a time his life seemed in danger; and when at last Cape Wiapoco (now Cape Orange) was sighted, he was unable to rise from his bed to look at the welcome land. The ships coasted along for three days, and on the 14th November Ralegh had himself carried on shore at Caiana (now the river Cayenne). He pined for fresh air, and change from his uncomfortable sick-bed on board the ship, which was in a frightful state from the sickness and death of so many men.

Ralegh's first thought on nearing land was to inquire for his former Indian servants. These men had looked eagerly for his return, and had boarded the ships which had come from England under Keymis, Leigh, and Harcourt, in anxious hope of finding him. One of them, Harry by name, had been with him in England; and after living two years in the Tower with him, had gone back to his own country. He now sent provisions beforehand by his brother to announce his coming. He had forgotten most of his English, but not his love for his old master. He brought with him bread, and plenty of fresh meat and fruit, which Ralegh did not at first dare to eat, on account of his state of health. But he began by degrees to gather a little strength. Though it was thirteen years since he had been amongst them, the Indians had cherished his remembrance as that of the great cacique who had done no harm, but only brought them hope of happy days, and freedom from the hated Spaniards.

From Caiana Ralegh wrote to his wife: "Sweet-heart, I can yet write unto you with but a weak hand; for I have suffered the most violent calenture for fifteen days that ever man did and lived; but God, that gave me a strong heart, hath also now strengthened it in the hell-fire of heat." He went on to tell of the sickness and bad weather which had assailed them.   He spoke gratefully of the presents of the governor's wife, saying that without them he could not have lived.   He had preserved the fruit in fresh sand, and had some of it still, to his great refreshing.   There were a few joyful pieces of news in the letter for the wife and mother.   "Your son," wrote Ralegh, "had never so good health, having no distemper in all the heat under the line."   And again, "To tell you that I might be King of the Indians were a vanity; but my name hath still lived among them. Here they feed me with fresh meat, and all that the country yields; all offer to obey me."   This letter was taken home by one Captain Alley, who was obliged to return for his health.

In the safe harbour formed by the mouth of the river Caiana they refreshed themselves, cleaned and repaired their ships, took in water, and set up their barges.   On the 4th of December they again set sail, and had some difficulty in getting over the bar at the mouth of the river.   It had now become clear that Ralegh's state of health made it impossible for him to lead in person the expedition up the Orinoco in search of the mines. "Besides this impossibility," says Ralegh, in excuse of his not having gone, "neither would my son nor the rest of the captains and gentlemen have adventured themselves up the river (having but one month's victuals, and being thrust together a hundred of them in a small fly-boat), had I

Q

not assured them that I would stay for them
at Trinedado, except I were sunk in the sea or
set on fire by the Spanish galleons; for that they
would have adventured themselves upon any other
man's word or resolution, it were ridiculous to
believe." Both for the sake of his own health and
for the safety of the explorers, it was necessary
that Ralegh should stay with the chief body of
the fleet. No one else could be depended upon
with perfect security to await their return, whatever dangers might beset him.

Next came the difficult question, to whom the
command of the exploring party was to be given.
The only person in any way fitted to take it was
Captain Keymis. He was a brave and faithful
man, and knew the country well. But more was
wanted for such a difficult post; and Keymis,
though a faithful servant, was not an intelligent
commander. He was not able under difficult circumstances to choose the right course, and abide
by it; he was not able to look before, and see the
result of his actions. Still there was no one better,
and so the general command of the expedition was
given to him, while the land forces were put
under George Ralegh, a nephew of Sir Walter's,
under whom young Walter commanded a company.

On the 15th December Keymis, with the five
smaller vessels of the fleet, parted from Sir Walter
at the Triangle Isles. Ralegh gave him minute
instructions as to the course he was to pursue. It

was supposed that there was a Spanish town near
the mine. The explorers were to avoid this, and
encamp between the town and the mine. They
were then to examine the nature of the mine. If
it proved very rich, and the Spaniards began to
attack them, they were to drive back the Spaniards.
Ralegh had no fear of breaking the peace, if he
were sure of carrying home great riches. But if
the mine did not prove very rich, they were to
content themselves with carrying off one or two
basketsful, enough to satisfy James I. that the
mine really existed. On the other hand, if, as
seemed possible, a Spanish force had been sent,
in obedience to warnings from Madrid, to oppose
their approach to the mine, Keymis was to be
careful how he landed; "for," said Ralegh bitterly,
" I know (a few gentlemen excepted) what a scum
of men you have, and I would not for all the
world receive a blow from the Spaniards to the
dishonour of our nation." He concluded by promising that they would find him, on their return,
at Puncto Gallo, dead or alive. " If you find not
my ships there," he added, "you shall find their
ashes; for I will fire with the galleons, if it come
to extremity; but run away I will never."

So they parted. Better had it been for them if
they had never met again, if their worst fears had
been realized, if of Ralegh and his ships nothing
indeed had been left but the ashes, burnt after a
hopeless and desperate struggle with Spanish
galleons. But it was not so to be. There was

to be tragedy enough, but it was tragedy deeper than defeat in battle.

Ralegh spent the time of their absence in cruising about Trinidad, observing the nature of the coast and of the birds and flowers that were to be found there. On the 13th February his diary abruptly closes. It is probable that on the next day he heard news which even he had not sufficient courage to write down. What need was there to record the events of the voyage any longer ?

Keymis and his companions entered the Orinoco by its principal mouth, past Puncto Anegada (now Port Barima), and continued their journey up the river till the 1st January, when they reached the Island of Yaya (called Assapana by Ralegh). They passed on, hoping to reach the mine before the Spaniards could hear of their presence on the river. Great was their surprise when they perceived amongst the trees on the river bank a cluster of houses which was clearly a Spanish settlement. It was a new town of San Thome, which had sprung up since the English were last there, and consisted of 140 houses, or rather bamboo huts, with a church and two convents. They could not hope to pass on to the mine unseen by the Spaniards. Still to have gone on would have been far the wisest course. They might then have reached the mine, and there, if need be, have repelled the attack of the Spaniards. But here Keymis showed his want

of wisdom.   He began at once to land his men.
The Spaniards had been warned of their coming
by an Indian fisherman, and formed an ambus-
cade from which they attacked the English, but
were soon forced back upon San Thome.   In the
night of the 1st January, the English attacked
the town.   The Spaniards made a gallant defence, though they were very inferior in numbers.
They continued fighting till the English reached
the little open square in the middle of the town.
Then they threw themselves into the houses, and
fired upon their foes till the English set fire to
the houses, when they were forced to fly into the
forest.

Whilst the English were fighting their way into
San Thome, none had fought more bravely than
young Walter Ralegh ; he had been wounded, but
still pressed on, encouraging the rest, till a blow
felled him to the ground to rise no more.   His
last words were—" Go on ; may the Lord have
mercy upon me and prosper your enterprise."
So to gain a miserable little Spanish settlement,
where for all their searching the English could
find no treasure, this bright young life had been
lost, which was dearer far to Ralegh than all the
gold in Guiana.

The next day young Ralegh and four others who
had fallen were buried in the church.   All the
soldiers followed under arms, with muffled drums
beating, pikes trailing, and five banners carried
before them.   They laid their Admiral's son near

the altar, and this sad task done, there remained the question, What was to be done next? Keymis seems to have lost heart and courage. He started with two launches to go up the river in search of the mine; but he was attacked by some Spaniards, who killed nine of his men. He turned back to San Thome for more. His men were beginning to grow discontented, whilst the difficulties in his way increased daily. The Spaniards, who knew the country well, were watching his movements from the thick woods or the river bank, ready to spring upon him at any unguarded moment. How was he to reach the mine? and besides, What would be the good of finding it? He could neither hold it nor work it. It would only fall into the hands of the Spaniards. Even if he could take any gold safely back to England, it would only be seized by the King. Keymis gave way before the difficulties which beset him, and determined to go back to the ships. Before he did so, George Ralegh made an expedition up the river for one hundred and ten leagues, with a view of examining the fitness of the country for colonization. He was struck with its rich resources; but amongst the crowd of discontented men at San Thome, the scum of the whole earth, as Ralegh called them, there were none capable of sharing his views. He found them on his return only more impatient to return. So at last they turned their backs on the mine and dropped down the river again, leaving San Thome in ashes, and carrying with them only the small amount of booty they had found in the town.

Keymis had already sent the sad tidings of young Walter's death to the Admiral by an Indian pilot. Now he brought the news of the total failure of the expedition. It was not to be expected that Ralegh would listen to his excuses with patience. What availed such feeble apologies when everything was lost, since Keymis had not even brought back a basketful of gold to prove that the mine existed? Ralegh listened to him with growing anger, and at last burst forth—" It is for you to satisfy the King, since you have chosen your own way. I cannot do it." Keymis had been full of remorse before, and grew more and more dispirited as he tried in vain during two wretched days to convince either himself or his Admiral that he had acted rightly. He had lost his old master's confidence, he had ruined Ralegh's credit, as Ralegh bitterly told him. At last he wrote a letter in excuse of his conduct to the Earl of Arundel, who had been one of the chief promoters of the enterprise, and brought it to Ralegh. Ralegh would not look at it. "You have undone me," he said, " by your folly and obstinacy, and I will not favour or colour in any sort your former folly." Keymis asked sadly if this was his final resolution; and when Ralegh said it was, Keymis said, as he turned towards his cabin, "I know then what course to take."

A little while afterwards the report of a pistol

was heard, and Ralegh sent a boy to ask what had happened. Keymis called out from his cabin to the boy that he had fired the shot to clean his arms. Half an hour afterwards the boy went into the cabin, and·found Keymis lying dead upon his bed, a long knife in his heart. The pistol had only broken a rib, and he had finished the work with his knife.

Discontent and mutiny were beginning to break out in the fleet. Ralegh would have liked still to make a desperate attempt to find the mine, but no one would second him. Letters had been found at San Thome from Madrid, warning the settlers of his coming. He felt as if he had been betrayed to the Spaniards, and he heard moreover that daily reinforcements from Spain were expected. If his men would not agree to face the risks of another attempt to find the mine, they might at least lie in wait for the Mexican fleet. But they would agree to nothing, and two ships even deserted him. The exact date on which he set sail from Trinidad is not known; but on March 21st he wrote to Winwood, of whose death in October he had not heard, from St. Christopher's in the Antilles. He had nothing to write of, he said, "than of the greatest and sharpest misfortunes that have ever befallen any man." After giving an account of all that had happened, he said, that had it not been for the desertion of the two ships, "I would have left my body at San Thome, by my son's, or have brought with me, out of that or other mines, so much gold ore as should have satisfied the King that I had propounded no vain thing. What shall become of me now I know not; I am unpardoned in England, and my poor estate consumed, and whether any other Prince or State will give me bread I know not." To his wife he wrote, "I was loathe to write, because I knew not how to comfort you; and God knows I never knew what sorrow meant till now. . . . . Comfort your heart, dearest Bess; I shall sorrow for us both. I shall sorrow the less because I have not long to sorrow, because not long to live. . . . . My braines are broken; it is a torment for me to write, and especially of misery."

Ralegh seems to have gone to Newfoundland on his way home. The fleet met with much rough weather; the men were discontented and mutinous; and when Ralegh reached Plymouth, on the 21st of June, his ship, the *Destiny*, was alone; the other ships had deserted him.

CHAPTER XVI

The Execution of Sir Walter Ralegh.

THE news of the doings of the English on the Orinoco had reached London in the second week of May. Sarmiento was at once loud in his complaints to the King of Ralegh's conduct. James was quite ready to listen to him, and to agree with him that Ralegh had been the first to break the peace. On the 9th of June he issued a proclamation, inviting all persons who might be able to supply information about the doings of Ralegh and his fleet to come and give evidence before the Privy Council. In the proclamation he spoke of the "horrible invasion of the town of San Thome," and of "a malicious breaking of the peace which hath been so happily established, and so long inviolately continued." James showed himself all eagerness to propitiate Spain; and his conduct makes it all the more wonderful that he should ever, thinking as he did, have allowed the expedition to start at all. No sane man can have supposed that Ralegh would have been allowed to get possession of a mine, situated in a territory

which the Spaniards claimed as their own, and in
which they had made settlements, without having
some fighting with the Spaniards.

Ralegh has been blamed for having gone on the
expedition, promising that he would not break the
peace, whilst he clearly meant to do so. In so
doing, there was in his mind no attempt to de-
ceive. He still held to the view current in Elizabethan days of "No peace beyond the line." To
fight with the Spaniards, who had been guilty of
putting to death with horrible cruelty English
merchants who had come merely to trade with
them, was no crime in his eyes. He was firmly
persuaded that if he could only bring back gold,
or even clear proof of the existence of the mine,
James, with his empty treasury, would willingly
pardon the death of a few Spaniards. In the
days when he and Drake and Hawkins had sailed
the seas before, Elizabeth had not made too curious
inquiries whether they broke the peace. He did
not understand this new spirit of truckling to the
Spaniard. True, it was not wise to go under the
circumstances. But after those thirteen years in
the damp, gloomy Tower, were not a few whiffs
of fresh sea air worth any risk? What wonder
if he grew careless, caught at everything, promised anything, if only he might be allowed once
more to try to do something?

As soon as she heard that the *Destiny* had
reached Plymouth, Lady Ralegh hastened to meet
her husband; and sad must the meeting have

been for both, whilst the future grew more gloomy
to Ralegh as he heard of the way in which the
King had received the tidings of his doings.   He
left Plymouth, on his way to London, in the
second week of July, his wife and one of his
officers, Captain King, going with him.   They had
not gone more than twenty miles when they met
Sir Lewis Stukeley, Vice-Admiral of Devon, who
said that he had orders to arrest both Sir Walter
and his ships.   They had to turn back to Plymouth
together.   Stukeley treated Sir Walter as a friend;
for he wished to gain his confidence, and so learn
his secrets.   At Plymouth Ralegh lodged with his
wife and King in a private house, whilst Stukeley
was busy looking after the ship.   Lady Ralegh,
in her fear for the future, pleaded anxiously with
her husband that he would try to escape.   King
joined in her pleading.   At last Ralegh yielded
to them, and King engaged a vessel to carry him
to France.   At midnight Ralegh and King started
in a little boat to row to the vessel.   But when
they were within a quarter of a mile of it Ralegh
gave orders to turn the boat round.   Before he
sailed for Guiana he had solemnly promised
Arundel and others that he would come back.
By merely landing at Plymouth he had not kept
his word.   He would not fly.   He allowed King
to give orders that the vessel should be kept in
readiness for another night or two; but he did not
try to get to her again.   He preferred to be true
to his word, and come back to face his accusers.

Stukeley was busy selling the tobacco with which the *Destiny* had been laden; but on the 25th of July, in obedience to an order from the council, he started for London with his prisoner. They passed through country well known to Ralegh, which must have wakened many fond recollections. They went close by the fair woods and pastures of Sherborne, which he had hoped to leave to his children for ever; and the men of Devon and Dorset, who knew and loved him well, must have crowded to gaze on him as he passed.

Ralegh was very anxious to gain some time before reaching London. Time was wanted to enable his friends to prepare to do for him all that they could; and he himself wished to write, whilst it was possible, a statement of his doings in Guiana to send to the King. He felt that his condition was very desperate. The next day, after passing Sherborne, when near to Salisbury, he got out to walk down the hill, and drew Manourie, a French doctor, who was one of their company, aside, and began to speak to him of his desire to gain time, " in order," he said, " that I may work my friends, give order for my affairs, and, it may be, pacify his Majesty before my coming to London; for I know well that, as soon as I come there, I shall to the Tower, and that they will cut off my head, if I use no means to escape it." He proceeded to ask Manourie to give him an emetic, so that he might counterfeit illness, which would make a delay necessary. That night, at Salisbury, he complained of headache and giddiness. The next morning early he sent his wife, with King and her servants, on to London, so that they might lose no time in doing all they could for him. King was commissioned to hire a ship in London or Gravesend, to lie in readiness to take Sir Walter to France, should there be any opportunity of escape.

Shortly after they had gone Ralegh feigned to be seized with a fit, so that his servant rushed into Stukeley's room, crying, "My master is out of his wits. I have just found him in his shirt upon all fours, gnawing at the rushes on the boards." Manourie was sent to see if he could do anything for Ralegh, and gave him the emetic which he had asked for. To make the deception still more complete, Manourie also gave Ralegh an ointment, which produced blisters and sores on any part of the skin to which it was applied. Seeing him in this condition, Stukeley thought he must indeed be seriously ill, and sent in all haste to the Bishop's Palace, where Andrewes, the saintly bishop of Ely, was then staying. Andrewes sent two physicians to see Ralegh, and they, together with Manourie, stated that he was unfit to go on with his journey.

The expedient appears to us quite unworthy of Ralegh; but he does not seem either then or subsequently to have felt any shame about it. Speaking of it afterwards, he said, "I hope it was no sin. The prophet David did make himself a fool . . .

and to him it was not imputed as a sin." The time he had thus gained he employed in writing his *Apology* for the voyage to Guiana. This, even under those strange circumstances, was written with glowing eloquence and is full of bitter scorn of his enemies. It shows us, more clearly than anything else that he afterwards said, his own point of view about the matter. For in it he states clearly the question as it then appeared to him, before he had heard the comments and accusations of others. On the fourth day of Ralegh's stay at Salisbury, James, who was then on progress, arrived in the town. Ralegh may have cherished some slight hope that he would be allowed to see the King. But a council warrant ordered that he should proceed on his journey immediately. Digby, who was with the King, heard that he was ill, and obtained permission for him on reaching London to go to his own house in Bread Street, instead of to the Tower.

On the way up to London Sir Walter, according to statements made afterwards by Manourie, talked much to him of plans for escape, and offered to pay him liberally if he would help him to do so. Manourie's statements are made rather incredible by the fact that Sir Walter was an impoverished man, and hardly in the position to offer Manourie fifty pounds a year as a reward for his assistance. Sir Lewis Stukeley now thought it wise to gain Ralegh's confidence by affecting deep pity for him, and a desire to help him in every way.

They reached London on August 7th, and Ralegh remained in his own house in Bread Street under the charge of Stukeley. Here Captain King came to him, and told him that he had made arrangements for a vessel now lying at Tilbury to take him over to France. Stukeley professed himself perfectly willing to aid him to escape, and to go to France with him. Two Frenchmen, by name Chesnay and Le Clerc, also came to Ralegh, with offers of assistance. They said that they had letters of recommendation which they would give him to different persons in France, and that they would put a French barque at his disposal. Ralegh accepted the letters, but thought that the barque provided by King would be more suitable for his purpose. Meanwhile Hart, the owner of the boat, had betrayed the whole scheme to a certain Herbert, a courtier, who had told it to some one else, who had informed the King. Arrangements were made, not to prevent the attempt to escape altogether, but only to prevent it from succeeding, so that to the other charges against Ralegh the charge of having tried to escape might be added.

Stukeley played the traitor to such perfection that he was rewarded afterwards by the indignant English with the name of "Judas," and was commonly known as Sir Judas Stukeley. On Sunday evening, 9th August, Ralegh, King, Stukeley, and one or two servants who were to be of the party, met on the river side. Two wherries, under the charge of Hart, were in readiness to convey them to the vessel, which lay at Gravesend. Another boat also lay near by, in which was Herbert, with a large crew. This boat followed them at a distance as they put out, and excited Sir Walter's suspicions. Stukeley was indignant with him for doubting, and with many oaths exclaimed against his bad fortune in having adventured his life with a man so full of doubts and fears. Doubts and misgivings delayed them so that they lost the advantage of the tide. The watermen said they would not be able to reach Gravesend till morning. The other boat meanwhile still followed them. From the conduct of Hart it at last became so clear to Ralegh that he had been betrayed, that he ordered the boats to turn and row back, in hopes that he might reach his house before morning, and nothing be known of his attempt to escape. Stukeley continued to assure him of his friendship, and even went so far as to embrace him in the boat, with vehement protestations of love. At Greenwich he persuaded Ralegh to land, saying he durst not take him to his house. Herbert and his men landed at the same time. Here Stukeley tried to persuade King that it would be better for his master if King should pretend that he had betrayed Ralegh, but to this the sturdy sailor would not agree. At last Stukeley gave up the deception, arrested King, and gave him over to some of Herbert's men. Ralegh seems to have been neither indignant nor surprised at such treachery; but only said to Stukeley, "Sir Lewis, these actions will

R

not turn out to your credit," words which were to prove truer even than Ralegh thought. In the morning, as they were led into the Tower, Ralegh found opportunity for a few words of comfort to King. "Stukeley has betrayed me; for your part you need be in fear of no danger; but as for me, it is I am the mark that is shot at."

When Ralegh was taken into the Tower his person was searched, and all the jewels and trinkets which were found on him were given over to Stukeley. Ralegh was a great lover of jewels, and there seem to have been some fine ones on his person; amongst others a diamond ring, which he always wore on his finger, and which had been given him by Queen Elizabeth. There were besides upon him sixty-three gold buttons, with sparks of diamonds; a jacinth seal, with a figure of Neptune cut on it; a loadstone in a scarlet purse; a Guiana idol of gold and silver, and many other trinkets. There was also a miniature in a case set with diamonds, which, at Sir Walter's express desire, was left in the hands of the Lieutenant of the Tower, Sir Allen Apsley. Beside these jewels, Stukeley obtained afterwards, as payment for his services with regard to Ralegh, £965.

Six councillors were now appointed as a commission to inquire into Ralegh's case. Amongst these were Bacon, Coke, and Abbot, the Archbishop of Canterbury. They held many sittings, and Ralegh was thrice examined before them. Many other persons were also examined, chiefly

men who had been on the Guiana expedition.
We still possess the results of some of their
examinations, from which we are able to see the
points upon which the commissioners especially
desired information. These were, whether Sir
Walter Ralegh really believed in the existence of
the mine, and meant to go there, and to work it;
whether he himself had directed that the Spanish
town should be burnt; whether he would have
sailed from Trinidad, had his officers allowed it,
and deserted those who had gone up the Orinoco;
whether he meant to turn pirate, and what was
the nature of his relations with France. To gain
still more information, a keeper, named Sir Thomas
Wilson, was appointed to attend on Ralegh in the
Tower, to be with him constantly, to win his confidence, and try to discover something from him.
He was to inform the commissioners of anything
he thought worth reporting. Wilson entered upon
his hateful office on the 10th of September, and
gave it up on the 15th October, when there seemed
no chance of learning anything more. He inter-
cepted Ralegh's letters; and means were even
found by Secretary Naunton to persuade Lady
Ralegh to write, asking certain questions of her
husband, in the hope that through his answers
more might be discovered.

At last, on the 18th October, the commissioners'
report was sent in to the King. It seems to have
been drawn up by Coke, but represented the views
of the whole body. The difficulty of the case was,

that as Ralegh had already, in 1604, been declared
guilty of high treason, and had never been par-
doned, he could not be put on his trial for any
crime committed since, as he was legally dead.
The commissioners, therefore, recommended two
courses as possible. The first, that in publishing the
warrant for Ralegh's execution, his Majesty should
also publish a narrative in print of his late crimes
and offences. The second course, and the one preferred by the commissioners, was that Sir Walter
should be summoned before the whole body of
the Council of State and the principal judges, together with some of the nobility and gentlemen of
quality, and should be thus publicly charged with
acts of hostility, depredation, abuse of the royal
commission, attempt to escape, and the other
misdemeanours of which he stood accused. The
commissioners left it to his Majesty how far the
matter with the French should be touched upon;
for their careful examination of the Frenchmen
who had had dealings with Ralegh led them to the
conclusion that he had been passive rather than
active in the matter. After the examination, the
King was to take the advice of the Lords of the
Council and the Judges as to the execution of
Sir Walter, and the whole proceeding was to be
made a solemn act of the council.

James was afraid to follow their advice. "For
the other course," he wrote in answer, "of a public
calling him before our council, we think it not fit,
because it would make him too popular, as was

found by experiment at the arraignment at Winchester, where by his wit he turned the hatred of men into compassion of him." James therefore resorted to a middle course. A formal proceeding was to take place, but only before the commissioners; no publicity was to be allowed. The sentence of his execution, which had been so long suspended, was then to be carried into effect; after which a declaration was to be put forward in print, stating the crimes of which he had been found guilty. On one point James was very determined; Ralegh must lose his life. He owed it to Spain that the man who had broken the peace and burnt a Spanish town should not be spared. The Spaniards had long looked upon Ralegh as their bitter foe. James had written to Madrid, offering to give up Ralegh for execution there. On the 15th October he received the answer that Philip III. would prefer that the execution should be in England, and that he hoped it would take place immediately.

In England many were found to intercede for Ralegh; amongst others, Queen Ann, who wrote to Villiers, now Duke of Buckingham, addressing him as "My kind dog," and asking him to exert his influence with the King to prevent Ralegh's execution. Ralegh himself wrote to Buckingham a somewhat fawning letter, begging him to do what he could to get his Majesty's pardon for him. To Lord Carew, his cousin, he wrote a long and dignified letter, in which he justified

his doings by his favourite argument, that Guiana
belonged to the English crown by virtue of the
cession made to him in 1595; so that the Spaniards
had no right to be there at all. From this letter,
and from his *Apology*, it is easy to see what was
Ralegh's view about the matter. He did not
believe in "peace beyond the line," and could not
understand how other people could believe in it.
His early training had taught him to look upon
the Spaniard as a foe who must be resisted at
any price. It may be urged that he had dis-
tinctly undertaken not to break the peace; but
he must have thought that this was only exacted
as a matter of form. Since every one knew that
he was bound for Guiana, and every one knew
that there were already Spanish settlements there,
no one could suppose that a collision could be
avoided. Elizabeth's subjects had always resisted
the Spanish claims to supremacy in the Indies,
and had looked upon it as lawful to win from
Spain, by fair fighting, all the booty they could.
The Spaniards, in like manner, had treated all
Englishmen whom they met in the Indies as their
enemies, and had even put to death with horrible
tortures peaceable merchants with whom they had
been trading. In the true interests of colonization and commerce, it was necessary that this
state of things should cease; that the dealings of
one nation with another should be regulated by
the same rules in the Indies as they were in
Europe. This was what men were beginning to

think, and what made doings like the burning of St. Thome entirely unjustifiable to a legal mind like Bacon's. To Ralegh individually small blame can be attached, because he had failed to understand how men's feelings had changed during those thirteen years which he spent in the Tower. For the sake of liberty he had been over-ready to promise, and had trusted that some chance might turn up to favour his attempt. Looked at from a modern point of view, the capture and burning by an Englishman of a foreign settlement, belonging to a people with whom his nation was at peace, is an unjustifiable act. But in considering its bearing upon our judgment of Ralegh's character, we must remember the state of opinion under which he had grown up, and the circumstances of his life. In his eyes at least it was no crime, and he was astonished that others should think it so. In his eyes his only crime was the failure of his expedition.

James had put himself into a false position with regard to Spain by allowing the expedition to start at all. His one wish now was to give full satisfaction to Spain by the execution of the traitor. He knew it would be an unpopular act; and he was afraid of allowing Ralegh to be examined publicly. By refusing to do so he took the unwisest course he could possibly have done. He allowed Ralegh to be executed by virtue of the old sentence, which was still unrepealed, and did not first make clear to the public the reasons why the sentence was now allowed to take effect, after the lapse of fourteen years. In this way Ralegh appeared to every one as a martyr, and as a martyr to Spain, which was just then the object of popular hatred. Even those who at the present day are inclined to judge severely Ralegh's conduct, with regard to the Guiana expedition, can hardly defend either the fact or the manner of his execution.

With regard to his dealings with France, we see that the commissioners considered that his part in them was passive rather than active. He confessed them all to the King in a letter written from the Tower on the 5th October. What his dealings with Faige were before he went to Guiana we have already seen. After his return he had been visited three times by a French gentleman named Chesnay, and once by the French agent in London, Le Clerc, with offers of assistance. Much irritation had already been excited at the French court by the way in which Chesnay and Le Clerc had been examined before the commissioners. James thought therefore that this matter had better be only very lightly touched upon, doubtless through fear lest anything should arise in consequence to disturb his friendly relations with France.

On the 28th October Ralegh was summoned from the Tower to appear before the councillors at Westminster. As he passed out, an old servant of his reminded him that he had forgotten to comb his head. "Let them kem it that are to have it," answered Ralegh, smiling; and added, "Dost thou know, Peter, of any plaister that will set a man's head on again when it is off?"

In answer to the charges of the commissioners, Ralegh spoke out as fearlessly as ever. He pleaded that he could not be proceeded against on the old sentence, which had been annulled by the royal commission which he had received for his voyage, a voyage which, "notwithstanding my endeavours," he said, "had no other issue than what was fatal to me—the loss of my son, and the wasting of my whole estate." He indignantly affirmed his intention to find the mine, and denied that he had intended to abandon his fleet, or bring about war between Spain and England. At the end the commissioners declared that in their opinion the sentence might justly be proceeded with, and Sir Walter was ordered to prepare for death the next morning. He was conveyed from Westminster Hall to a small building in the Palace Yard, the gatehouse of the Old Monastery, which had long been used as a prison. As he passed across the yard he met an old friend, to whom he said, "You will come to-morrow morning." And when his friend answered, "Certainly," Ralegh added, "I do not know what you may do for a place. For my own part, I am sure of one; you must make what shift you can." Many came to see him in the gatehouse. One of his kinsmen, surprised at his good spirits, said, "Do not carry it with too much bravery. Your enemies will take exception if you do." "It is my last mirth in this world," answered Ralegh; "do not grudge it to me. When I come to the sad parting, you shall see me grave enough."

Ralegh had always professed scorn of death. Now he seemed to welcome it cheerfully as a friend. Dr. Robert Tounson, Dean of Westminster, was ordered by the Lords of the Council to be with him during his last night in prison, and at his death. Tounson says in a letter which he wrote to a friend about Ralegh's bearing at his death, "he was the most fearless of death that ever was known, and the most resolute and confident, yet with reverence and conscience. When I began to encourage him against the fear of death, he seemed to make so light of it that I wondered at him. . . He gave God thanks he never feared death; and much less then, for it was but an opinion and imagination; and the manner of death, though to others it might seem grievous, yet he had rather die so than of a burning fever, with much more to that purpose, with such confidence and cheerfulness, that I was fain to divert my speech another way, and wished him not to flatter himself; for this extraordinary boldness I was afraid sprang from some false ground. If it sprang from the assurance he had of the love and favour of God, of the hope of his salvation by Christ and his own innocency, as he pleaded, I said he was a happy man; but if it were out of an humour of vain glory, or carelessness, or contempt of death, or senselessness of his own estate, he were much to be lamented. For I told him that heathen men had set as little by their lives as he could do, and seemed to die as bravely. He answered that he was persuaded that no man that knew God and feared Him could die with cheerfulness and courage, except he was assured of the love and favour of God unto him; that other men might make shows outwardly, but they felt no joy within; with much more to that effect very Christianly, so that he satisfied me then, as I think he did all his spectators at his death."

That night Lady Ralegh came to the gatehouse to bid farewell to her husband. Till midnight they talked together. Of his son Carew he could not bear to talk to her, but he told her how she must try to vindicate his fame before the world if he should be prevented from making an address on the scaffold as he intended. Lady Ralegh told him that the Council had given her the disposal of his dead body. "It is well, dear Bess," he answered, " that thou mayst dispose of that dead which thou hadst not always the disposing of when alive."

That night, too, Ralegh employed himself in writing a testamentary note, in which he once more vindicated himself from the charges which had been brought against him. Then, too, he in all probability wrote some lines which were afterwards found in his Bible.

"When such is time that takes on trust
    Our youth, our joys, our all we have,

And pays us but with earth and dust;
Who in the dark and silent grave,
When we have wandered all our ways,
Shuts up the story of our days;
But from this earth, this grave, this dust,
My God shall raise me up, I trust."

Early in the morning he received the Communion. "He was very cheerful and merry," says Dr. Tounson, " and hoped to persuade the world that he died an innocent man as he said. He eat his breakfast heartily, and took tobacco, and made no more of his death than if it had been to take a journey."

The execution was to take place early. It was the Lord Mayor's day; and it had been hoped that the counter attraction of the show in the city would draw away many from hearing Sir Walter's last words. But the crowd in the yard was dense, and Ralegh, escorted by two sheriffs and Dr. Tounson, was so much thronged and crowded on his way to the scaffold that he was made quite breathless. One old bald-headed man pressed up towards him, and Ralegh asked him if he would aught of him. The man answered that he only wished to see him, and prayed God to have mercy upon his soul. Sir Walter thanked him, and taking off a nightcap of cut lace from his head threw it to him, with the words, "Take this; you need it, my friend, more than I do." On reaching the scaffold Ralegh said that he had been suffering from ague on the two last days; "If therefore," he added, "you perceive any weakness in me ascribe it to my sickness rather than to myself. I am infinitely bound to God, that he hath vouchsafed me to die in the sight of so notable an assembly, and not in darkness, neither in that Tower where I have suffered so much adversity and a long sickness." A number of lords, amongst whom were Arundel and Oxford, were watching the scene from a window in a dwelling-house which overlooked the yard. Turning to them, Ralegh said he wished his voice were strong enough for them to hear him. They answered that they would come down, and came and stood upon the scaffold. After they had shaken him by the hand, he began to speak again. He solemnly denied that he had had any plot or intelligence with the French king, or that he had spoken dishonourably and disloyally of King James. He called God to witness to the truth of these assertions. "It is not now a time," he said, "either to fear or to flatter kings. I am now the subject of death, and the great God of heaven is my sovereign before whose tribunal I am shortly to appear. And therefore have a charitable conceit of me. . . . . To call God to witness an untruth is a sin above measure sinful; but to do it at the hour of one's death . . . were the greatest madness and sin that could be possible." He said that in taking the Sacrament that morning he had forgiven both Stukeley and the Frenchman (Manourie). He confessed that he had tried to escape. He once more asserted his belief in the existence of the mine, and said that he had always meant to come home, however his voyage turned out. Turning to Arundel, he said, " I am glad my Lord Arundel is here;" and he told how he promised Arundel before he sailed that he would come back again, and had given him his hand upon it; and this Arundel confirmed. At the end Ralegh spoke a few words to justify himself of a charge made long ago against him, which he said made his heart bleed; namely, that he had been a persecutor of Essex, and had watched his execution from a window, with disdain puffing out tobacco. " God I take to witness," he said, " my eyes shed tears for him when he died. . . . I confess I was of a contrary faction; but I knew that my Lord of Essex was a noble gentleman, and that it would be worse for me when he was gone. . . ." Finally, Ralegh desired all " very earnestly to pray for him; for that he was a great sinner for a long time, and in many kinds his whole course was a course of vanity. A seafaring man, a soldier, and a courtier, the least of these were able to overthrow a good mind and a good man."

Then the executioner knelt and asked him forgiveness, which he granted, laying his hands upon the man's shoulders. He asked to see the axe, and as he felt its sharp edge, he said, " This gives me no fear; it is a sharp and fair pencil to cure me of all my distempers." Turning again to the executioner, he added, " When I stretch forth my hands despatch me."

Then with courtly grace he bade farewell to his friends who stood around, and turned with parting salutations to the crowd on either side of the scaffold, begging them heartily that they would give him their prayers. The executioner cast down his own cloak, and Ralegh laid himself upon it, and stretched forth his hands as a sign that he was ready; but the man hesitated. "What dost thou fear? Strike, man, strike!" said Ralegh, without stirring. His lips moved as if in prayer, and at last the axe fell; there were two blows, and the head rolled off.

When the head was lifted up and shown to the people, one man was heard to say, "We have not such another head to be cut off." The head was put into a red bag, and the body was wrapped in its velvet gown. They were carried to Lady Ralegh. She had asked her cousin, Sir Nicholas Carew, for permission to bury, in his church at Beddington, the dead body of her noble husband, "which the Lords had given her, though they had denied her his life." But for some reason or other she changed her mind, and had it buried near the altar of St. Margaret's Church, Westminster. She caused the head to be embalmed, and kept it with her till she died.

The way in which Ralegh met death—with the grace of a courtier, the dignity of a philosopher, the courage of a soldier, and the faith of a Christian—had made him more than ever a hero and a martyr in the eyes of the people. Sir John

Eliot, who afterwards himself suffered nobly in the people's cause, was present as a young man at his execution, and says, "His bearing left only this doubt, whether death was more acceptable to him, or he more welcome to death." From the report that is left us of his last words, scanty and insufficient as it necessarily is, we cannot judge the effect they produced. We can better judge of their eloquence from the way in which we are told they stirred the hearts of those who heard them. Afterwards the town could talk of nothing else. Every day ballads and pamphlets relating to Ralegh were published. Men looked upon him as having been unjustly executed under his old sentence, and fully accepted his own vindication of the charges since brought against him. The publication of the official declaration, which was to set forth the reasons why he had been executed, was for some reason or other delayed; indeed, men were so rooted in their opinions that it was hardly likely to produce any change; still less so, coming as late as it did.

Sir Judas Stukeley, as he was called, became the object of such bitter hatred that he did not know where to hide himself to escape from it. He is said to have died a raving maniac, despised and hated by all men. He had tried to excuse himself by writing an *Apology*, but men had not accepted it.

The official declaration of the causes which had led to Sir Walter Ralegh's death was drawn up by

Bacon, at the King's command. It contained a
recital of those charges which in the minds of the
commissioners had been proven against him. It
took for granted that Ralegh had never really
known of the existence of the mine that he had
pretended to go in search of; and starting from
this, it naturally found him guilty of having in
every way violated his commission. There can
be no doubt that Ralegh did go beyond his commission; but it is equally clear that he never
believed that he was bound strictly to adhere to
it. Neither in his *Apology* nor in his address
from the scaffold does he speak as if it had
ever occurred to him that his real fault was the
burning and sacking of San Thome. There does
not seem any reason to believe that the commissioners themselves looked upon this as his chief
crime. Neither he nor any one else ever denied
that San Thome had been burnt. If that act in
itself had been looked upon at that time as so
severe a breach of the law of nations as it would
be considered now, there would have been no need
of all the examinations of Ralegh himself and his
fellow-adventurers, with a view of proving other
things against him. Of that he stood clearly
accused by his own mouth; but that was not
enough to condemn him in those days. To the
great mass of people it was no crime at all; and
in James's eyes it was only a crime because he
feared lest it might bring about a breach with
Spain. Even the official declaration did not lay

so much stress upon the burning of San Thome as it did upon the other charges, which posterity has clearly judged to be of no weight.

The declaration, though drawn up by the master hand of Bacon, and possessing all the advantages of his clear and lucid style, produced no effect upon the excited minds of men. The common view was, that Ralegh was executed under his old sentence simply to please Spain. Even Dean Tounson expressed his surprise that Ralegh before his death never made mention of that for which he really died, his former treason.

Perhaps it is easier to forgive James I. Ralegh's execution than it is to forgive him the thirteen years' imprisonment in the Tower. When Sir Walter was executed, at the age of sixty-six, he was broken in health, and worn out with the labours and troubles of his eventful career. Life could have little more in store for him, and death on the scaffold gave him an opportunity of showing the world, in a way which it has not forgotten, how nobly a man can die. But when James came to the throne Ralegh was still in the prime of life, and no man then living was better fitted to do good work for his country. That James should have failed to make use of the noblest spirit amongst his people shows in a striking manner his incapacity for sympathizing with true genius.

Young amongst the heroes who gathered round Elizabeth's throne, Ralegh lived on into an age when genius was feared, not sought for. It is impossible to say what he might not still have done for his country, had he been allowed; it is difficult to say in a few words what he actually did. His manysidedness is the most striking thing about him, and by virtue of it he seems to sum up in himself all the leading characteristics of the Elizabethan age. A fearless soldier, a distinguished seaman, he was at the same time a most gallant and accomplished courtier. He could turn a compliment as gracefully as Sir Christopher Hatton, and attack a Spanish galleon as dauntlessly as Drake. Amongst the many great names in the literature of that age, his has found a worthy place as poet, philosopher, and historian. All his life a complete master of the intricacies of foreign politics, he took also, as long as he was able, an active and intelligent share in home politics. He delighted in far-reaching schemes, and saw how England was fitted, by her position and by the character of her people, to send forth offshoots into distant lands. To him we may look back as the father of English colonization.

But whilst busied in great schemes he did not forget the duties which lay near at hand. He administered the offices which he held under Elizabeth with zeal and care; he watched with deep interest the planting of his own estate; he never forgot to care for the faithful servants who had followed him through many dangers. By the introduction of the potato and tobacco he contributed largely to the comfort of his countrymen.

His chemical studies show how anxious he was to alleviate human suffering as much as he could. A self-summed man, of arrogant and overbearing manners, unable to contain the scorn which he felt for mean and common things, he was never loved by the people till his sufferings had taught them the real meaning of his character. The tide of popular feeling was turned at his trial at Winchester; and since then the English people have loved and honoured him amongst their heroes.

INDEX

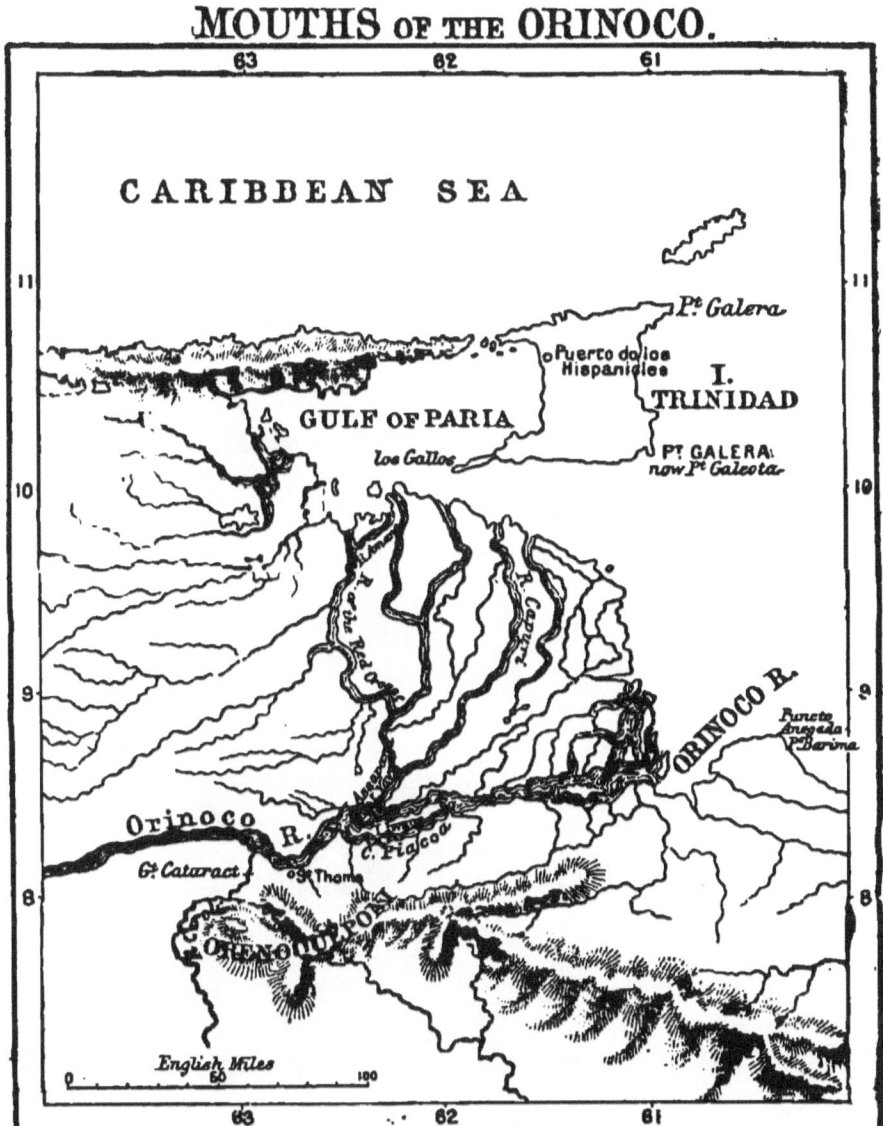

CARIBBEAN SEA

Pt Galera

o Puerto de los
Hispanioles

I.
TRINIDAD

GULF OF PARIA

Los Gallos

Pt GALERA
now Pt Galeota

ORINOCO R.

Punta
Anegada
P.ta Barima

Orinoco   R.

C. Piacoa

Gt Cataract

o St Thome

ORINOCO DELTA

English Miles

NORTH AMERICA

Newfoundland

VIRGINIA
CAROLINA
FLORIDA

Chesapeak Bay
Roanoke Island
Southern Island
Wocokon · Bermuda

West Indies

Trinidad
Orinoco R.
Triangle Isles
Calana or Cayenne
Cape Wiapoco
or Orange

GUYANA

SOUTH AMERICA

Fayal · · Tercira
Azores

Madeira
Lancerota
Canaries

IRELAND
SCOTLAND
Imewich
ENGLAND
FRANCE
SPAIN
Cadis

80   60   40   20   0

40

20

0

20

40

60

N
S

English Miles
250   500   1000